T0127419

# The Hanging in the Foaling Barn

# THE
# HANGING
## IN THE
# FOALING BARN

### STORIES
## Susan Starr Richards

Sarabande Books

LOUISVILLE, KENTUCKY

FIRST EDITION

No part of this book may be reproduced without written permission of the publisher. Please direct inquiries to:

Managing Editor
Sarabande Books, Inc.
2234 Dundee Road, Suite 200
Louisville, KY 40205

LIBRARY OF CONGRESS CATALOGING-IN-PUBLICATION DATA

Richards, Susan Starr, 1938–
    The hanging in the foaling barn : stories / by Susan Starr Richards.
        p.    cm. — (Woodford Reserve series in Kentucky literature)
    ISBN 1-932511-33-4 (pbk. : alk. paper)
    1. Kentucky—Social life and customs—Fiction. 2. Horses—Breeding—Fiction. 3. Horse breeders—Fiction. 4. Horse farms—Fiction. I. Title. II. Series.
    PS3618.I34455H36 2006
    813'.6—dc22                                        2005016823

13-digit ISBN 978-1-932-51133-8

Cover image © 2005 by Don Ament. Used by permission.

Cover and text design by Charles Casey Martin

Manufactured in Canada
This book is printed on acid-free paper.
Sarabande Books is a nonprofit literary organization.

This is a work of fiction. All names, characters, and incidents are the product of the author's imagination. Any resemblance to real events or persons, living or dead, is entirely coincidental.

*The Hanging in the Foaling Barn* is the third title in
The Woodford Reserve Series in Kentucky Literature.

THE KENTUCKY ARTS COUNCIL

The Kentucky Arts Council, a state agency in the Commerce Cabinet, provides operational support funding for Sarabande Books with state tax dollars and federal funding from the National Endowment for the Arts, which believes that a great nation deserves great art.

*for Dick*

# Table of Contents

## ACKNOWLEDGMENTS

"The Hanging in the Foaling Barn," *The Thoroughbred Times*
(First Prize, National Fiction Contest). Anthologized in *Prize
Stories 1994, The O. Henry Awards,* Doubleday.

"The Ape in the Face," *Shenandoah.*

"Clarence Cummins and the Semi-Permanent Loan,"
anthologized in *Kentucky Renaissance,* Gnomon Press.

"Man Walking," *The Sewanee Review.*

"The Screened Porch," *The Southern Review.* Anthologized in
*New Stories from the South, The Year's Best, 1991,* Algonquin.

"The Murderer, the Pony, and Miss Brown to You,"
*The Thoroughbred Times.*

"Magic Lantern," *The Kenyon Review.*

"Grass Fires," *The Journal of Kentucky Studies.*

"Gawain and the Horsewoman," *The Journal of Kentucky Studies.*

I am grateful, first, to the late Andrew Lytle, my eternal fiction
teacher. I thank the Art Group for years of encouragement and
advice, and especially my lifelong friend and reader Mary Ann
Taylor-Hall, who suggested that I put this collection together for
the Woodford Reserve Series in Kentucky Literature. Thanks
also to Neil Rush, for technical support.

My gratitude to my publisher, Sarah Gorham, for all her hard
work and enthusiasm, and to the whole staff at Sarabande, for

their dedicated attention—especially to Kirby Gann and Kristina McGrath, my editors; to Chuck Martin, the book's designer; and to Nickole Brown and Betsey Reed, who get the word out.

Most of all, infinite thanks to my main fiction critic and wise horseman—my husband, Dick Richards, who warms me up, cools me out, and keeps me sound. His energy and imagination have built me a blissful life on my own wild writer's retreat—our two beautiful farms. Finally I thank all my good old horses, living and dead; they are the foundation of that life.

# The Hanging in the Foaling Barn

# THE
# HANGING
## IN THE
# FOALING BARN

Here it was three-thirty in the morning. Between foaling mares and nursing sick foals, Luther hadn't slept more than three hours straight in the last two weeks. Tonight, at last, everything looked quiet, and he had gotten to bed with the prospect of being able to stay there all night, for a change.

And then the nightman called up to tell Luther he was going to hang himself in the foaling barn.

Luther sat there a minute, still jumped up in bed thinking something serious was happening—a mare was ready to go, a foal had a fever.

"Tell you what, Maurice," he said at last. "If you want to die so damn much, why don't you just go in Brownie's stall and stand behind her and touch her once on the butt? You'd get your picture took in a hurry."

"Why Luther,"—Maurice's vague, startled voice—"she might just hurt me."

Luther smiled sweetly at the telephone. "That's true. You

3

probably wouldn't stand anywhere near the right spot, and she'd probably just kick you someplace internal and you'd crawl into the hallway and lay there all night turning blue, and I'd have to fight all the mares past you in the morning before I could even turn out."

Luther thought about it. "All right," he said. "Only for God's sake don't hang yourself in front of the foaling stall. Wiggy's been snorting and staring in there every evening, still looking for that dead meadowlark the cat left in the corner last week. She won't go in, and then she keeps looking in all the corners and snorting, and in the morning she runs over top of you trying to get out. She'll never relax enough to have that foal. And if she does, she'll probably think it's a dead meadowlark, she's so dumb."

Maurice wasn't talking. Luther raised his voice. "Not as dumb as you are, though, Maurice. You got to call up and want to kill yourself here in the middle of May. Couldn't you wait till June, at least, when foaling season's over?" He slammed the phone down. Then sighed.

When Luther had first known him, Maurice was leading apprentice at River Downs. He'd ridden a lot of winners for Luther over two summers there. Back in those days he had yellow hair like bright wheat straw, and those tall slender girls that always love jockeys leaning all over him. A strut to go with it, and a flat back in the saddle. And a way of waiting on a horse most bug boys had no knowledge of, sitting still till it told him to move, and then only moving to disappear into it as it ran, till it was all one beast, man and horse, running together at the wire. Luther had believed Maurice had a chance to make it at the real races. But even then he was drinking, and pretty soon the weight got to him. He was an exercise rider for a while, and then a groom, and then Luther lost track of him entirely. When

4

at last he showed up working at a gas station in town, still talking horses all the time, Luther had given him the night job for old time's sake. He still drank, of course, but then most nightmen did. He didn't smoke, at least, so he wasn't likely to burn the barn down. And he claimed to have nightmares so bad that he never would sleep at night. It might even have been true—in eleven years of foaling, he'd never missed a mare.

The only trouble was, toward the end of every foaling season, Maurice started considering suicide. Of course, that just made him normal. Everybody started thinking about killing themselves, or someone else, this time of the year. But Maurice would get into ways and means. One night he tried to drown himself by driving into the farm pond, but since it was just four feet deep, he'd only managed to drown his Chevrolet truck. Luther bought him an old car to replace it, and then the next spring he tried to ram the car into the big oak by the driveway. His aim wasn't too good, so he made several passes at it, and by the time he gave up, he'd taken out about a quarter of a mile of fairly new plank fencing, and let the barren mares loose all over the farm.

But he'd never tried to kill himself in the foaling barn. Luther found himself not just irritated but indignant at this. The foaling barn was where the heavy-in-foal mares came swinging in every day with their huge bellies swaying rhythmically, and the new foals staggered up on their feet for the first time and tried to kick somebody right away. Everything there wanted to live so much, was so full of life. That was why you always felt so bad when sometimes they didn't make it. To try to kill yourself in the foaling barn, Luther believed, was sacrilegious.

Of course, he never thought for a minute that Maurice had any real intention of doing it. "But he's fool enough that he might just accidentally get it done," he said to himself. He sighed again. His clothes were right there by the telephone, ready, waiting for some mare to call him up and say she was foaling, waiting for life to call him up, instead of some dummy saying he wanted to kill himself. "Hang on, Maurice," he said. Then laughed out loud, once.

A branch came out and slapped at Luther's arm as he jerked the truck around the corner by the woods. Luther slapped back at it. The yearling colts came swirling up, blazing white and green-eyed in the headlights, racing the truck down the fence at a dead run, sliding on their butts like baseball players to stop in a scramble half an inch short of busting through the gate for the second time this week. "That's right," he said. "Y'all keep trying to kill yourselves, too."

The lights were on in the barn hallway, a big floating square of light with the dark trees outside touching the roof. Grids of shadows in the squared-off reaches above. The mares looked up, big-eyed, interested, some of them speaking to him, ever-hopeful of extra grain rations. The tack room was empty. He called. No answer. But he heard a little shifting noise up in the loft, like something afraid to move and afraid to sit still. Maurice was up there, all right. He was sitting in the hay bales. Luther could just make out the top of his hair, which didn't look like wheat straw any more—like old grass hay, by now.

Luther went in the foaling stall to check on Wiggy. "She do any more digging?" he called up to Maurice.

Maurice didn't answer, for a while. "Been real quiet," he said at last. "Don't worry," he added, in his singsong, mournful voice. "You ain't going to need me tonight."

"What about that new baby? You see him pee yet?"

"I done wrote you a note about that." There it was, on the clipboard by the door, written in Maurice's own edifying style: "The colts kidney acted."

"Be with you in a minute, Maurice," Luther said. "My

6

kidney's about to act." He went into Twinkle's stall to pee. There she was, talking to her little sick baby, so happy to have it on its feet again and nursing on its own. Not a bit happier than he was, though, after getting the foal up every two hours for the last two days. Luther calmed down some as he stood there, listening to the foal slurp its milk. All around him were the mares, munching slow and peaceful in their stalls, and some lying down and talking in their sleep to their new foals that hadn't been born yet, the way they do toward the end, having baby dreams. And here it all was in the middle of green fields stretching out in the dark, and the fireflies outside going on-off, on-off, and the air smelling like a grape popsicle the way it always did down by the woods this time of year.

And there was Maurice hiding up in the loft, wanting to kill himself. Talk about racehorses being crazy. At least if a horse killed itself, it was really trying to do something else, playing or fighting or just running.

Luther started climbing up the ladder, cursing silently as he maneuvered himself over the top. He did not like heights—not even the twelve-foot height of the loft.

A ragtag rope made of a bunch of shanks tied together looped up to the central two-by-eight above the hallway. At the other end of it was Maurice, huddled up on a hay bale like some stray cat waiting to be kicked, holding a makeshift noose in his hands. "Look at you," Luther said. "Forty-one years old. Still healthy, in spite of all the alcohol you've put in your system. Sitting up here on a hay bale wanting to hang yourself with a lead shank. Couldn't you just kindly wait a while? We ain't always going to be alive, you know."

Maurice said in a pitiful voice, "I waited long enough. I'm just doing what I should've done a long time ago."

"That's the truth," Luther said. "At least you sure should've done it before three-thirty in the morning. How come you didn't want to hang yourself just after supper? I had about twenty minutes then. I could've worked you in." Maurice was silent. The mares chewed, stopped, thought about it, chewed again. A foal whinnied in its sleep, jumped to its feet, its mama spoke to it softly. Maurice glanced out into the middle of the space above the hallway, as if he saw something there.

Luther didn't like that look. It reminded him a little of Crazy Harry, a horse that saw things—spooks—and no matter how many times you told him, "There ain't nothing there," he wouldn't believe you. He was always so sure there was something just up ahead of him that was going to jump on him that he would almost get you to believing it. Harry would freeze, and snort, and arch his neck, and bug his eyes, and start looking both ways to decide which way to bolt, till you'd find yourself saying, "What the hell is it? Where is it? What's it going to do?" You just couldn't pay attention to Harry at all, or he'd convince you the world really looked like he thought it did. What you had to do, Luther reminded himself, was to give him something else to think about.

"Suppose you get it done," he said, nodding at the rope, settling himself on the bale opposite Maurice. "Then what? How do you know you won't come right back again? How would you like that?"

Maurice stared at him kind of cock-eyed, the way he did. "Come back as a ghost, you mean? Ghosts can't feel nothing."

"But you'd remember feeling things. How it feels to be hanging in the middle of the barn, for example, with your head ripped loose from your body." Maurice hunched up a little bit more on his bale. Luther sank back on his. It was beginning to feel soft already.

He tried to calculate what he could do that would get him back home and to sleep quickest. He could hit Maurice on the head and tie him up with the shanks and leave him here until morning. Or he could leave him alone and let him jump. But that rope probably wouldn't hold, and he'd wind up just breaking his leg, and then Luther would have to do something with him in the morning. And anyway, Luther was against things breaking their legs in his barn. Even humans. Even Maurice.

"If only they hadn't taken me off of He's No Angel," Maurice said.

"Hell. They took you off that horse twenty years ago. And they didn't even take you off. You only rode him the once, remember? When that other boy had days?"

Maurice nodded dreamily. "He win by twenty. I never asked him for a thing. If I'd just stayed with him, I'd be riding in New York today."

Luther shut his eyes, feeling sleep right there behind his eyelids, dark and soft. "Yeah, and if things were different, I'd be Breeder of the Year. But I ain't planning to hang myself about it. What you need to do is to cool out a little. Life ain't all that serious to be worth killing yourself about."

Maurice was silent again for a while. Then, "You remember that time I win on Circus Cat?" he asked.

Luther grinned, reluctantly. This was one Maurice could always get him in on. Circus Cat was one of Luther's all-time favorite horses—not the best he'd ever bred, but probably the bravest—a tiny little filly who ran against the older horses at marathon distances on the local tracks, sometimes fifty lengths out of it in the backstretch, always hopelessly beaten going into the turn, and more often than not on top at the wire. In the race Maurice was talking about, even the winner's circle photographer had been faked out—she was still second when he took the picture of them all running at the end. Luther himself had turned away, saying, "Not this time," sure she was second, till he heard the shout as they put her number up.

"You remember what that guy said about her afterward?"

They recited it together, as wondering and staccato as the trainer of the second horse had said it after the race, shaking his head in disbelief. "That-sucker-came-from-freaking-Tennessee!"

"She did, too," Maurice said. "I can still feel it."

Luther could see it, himself—the filly still trailing the field when she came out of the final turn, then burrowing into the pack until she was almost invisible, just an impression of speed, a bay shadow, slipping sketchily through all those great big solid horses that seemed twice her size, to emerge third as the two leaders ran for the win. Then disappearing again between those two, then suddenly there, diving like a demon for the wire. "She was a wonderful little filly," he said softly. "You suited her down to the ground, too, Maurice. I have to say that."

Maurice nodded. His eyes had dropped to the rope again. "She was the last winner I was ever on. You put me on. When nobody else would. You was always good to me, Luther. And I let you down. I let everybody down. But I'm going to make it all up to you now. You ain't never going have to worry with me no more."

Luther leaned back against the hay bales. "Whatever you think, Maurice. I wouldn't want to tell a man his business. But all I want is to get back in the bed." He closed his eyes once, nodded, opened them again. He wasn't sure how long it had been. But Maurice had stood up, and he had the noose around his neck. He turned away toward the edge of the loft, holding his arms out from his sides as if he might explode. The rope lifted up a little around his neck; he tugged at it daintily with one finger. But he didn't move. "Standing tied," Luther said to himself.

Maurice straightened his shoulders. "I want to go," he said in a loud voice. "It's now or never." Then he stood there, as if waiting for something to happen.

"Looks like never to me," Luther said.

"Life don't make no sense," Maurice said, in a cracked,

inspired voice. Like he'd finally figured it out. "At least, my life don't. You think your life makes sense, Luther?"

Luther thought. "Not this part of it. Here I am sitting in a barn loft at four in the morning discussing life with a party who's planning to kill himself. What do you care?"

"That's right," Maurice said. He took a deep breath. He wiggled the rope around his neck once, like straightening a necktie. Then he started walking toward the edge of the loft. He was taking baby steps, but he was heading that way.

Luther growled. He got up and took two big steps and caught up with him. "Give me that," he said, reaching out to snag the noose. Maurice walked faster. "No. Stop, I tell you." He grabbed Maurice, turned him around. Maurice backed up. The rope pulled tight. Luther grabbed the rope. Maurice grabbed Luther. A slow waltz, Luther stepping forward, Maurice backward.

"Stop, now, what are you pulling on me for?"

"I ain't pulling. You're pushing. I want to do it. Just let me go on and jump."

"You ain't jumping. You're hanging on to me. Give me this rope, I tell you." They swung toward the edge of the loft together, their shadows huge, flapping against the light.

"Take that thing off your neck, now." Luther was breaking a sweat. "Here. Don't crowd me, you crazy booger. I ain't going to jump with you. This ain't no lover's leap." He was on the edge with his back to it, the space opening dizzily in the back of his head. They teetered outward together, and for a moment he was sure they were going over flat-out, heading for a great big double belly-whopper on the floor of the barn. Then they teetered back again.

Luther lunged forward, swung Maurice around with one big jerk of his arms. His heart was pounding wildly.

Now Maurice stood with his back to the opening. He still had a stranglehold on Luther. His eyes, close up, were blood-red, filling Luther's vision, like the eyes of a horse that has been in the stall too long and is fighting you to get out, banging on the walls, climbing all over you. Luther wrestled himself loose and stepped back.

But then it was as if all that red had gotten in his own eyes. He saw Maurice crouched before him, looking strange, black lines running all over his face, like a cup about to crack. Talking in a funny, screechy voice, saying "Don't, Luther,"or "No, Luther," or "Whoa, Luther," over and over again. Behind him was the great complex orderly opening above the hallway. Luther could feel the push coming all the way from his heels, could see Maurice rocketing off into the clean space behind him.

Then there was a big blow in Luther's middle, like he'd been kicked. And he was sitting on the floor, alone in the loft. And the rope was holding. It was swinging back and forth like a pendulum, while Luther watched it in disbelief, certain that Maurice had to be the weight at the other end of it, since nothing else could be, but trying hard to think of some other explanation. The rope stopped swinging and started jiggling, twitching, like someone was fishing with it. There was an unfamiliar noise, coming with the twitches; grunts of effort, it sounded like. The rope's motions got tighter and tighter, the grunts got louder and louder. His breath knocked out, sucking for air himself, Luther could only listen respectfully. Was it that much work—hanging?

Then the whole barn seemed to shift, to get up and crawl a little under him. Maurice's hay-colored hair, sticking straight up, was reappearing over the strawy edge of the loft.

Now, when he had discussed the possibility of Maurice coming back from the dead with him a few minutes before, it had never occurred to Luther that he might really do it. The rope was still taut. It still held his weight, clearly, it still twitched and wiggled. But Maurice's hair was not down there at the end of it where it should have been. It was, somehow, bobbing or floating or flying back up toward the loft again, back toward Luther. And there was Maurice's whole head, staring at Luther over the edge. It opened its mouth several times to speak, but there was just a gurgle. At last it said, in a surprised, interested voice, "This mare's foaling." There was a little whistling sound, and the head disappeared again.

Luther sat there staring. Maurice had just come back from the dead to tell him his mare was foaling. Then he said, "What?" He jumped up and ran over to the edge. There was Maurice, all of him, head and arms and legs, wrapped around the rope, grinning up at Luther, looking livelier than Luther had seen him in years. "Hell, Maurice," Luther said. "You're going to have to do better than this. You ain't anywhere near dead." He grabbed hold of the rope and hauled Maurice in hand-over-hand, like a big fish, and they both scrambled back down the ladder.

And there was Wiggy, the silver birth-sack already sticking out of her like a great big light bulb. A front foot already visible in it. Luther walked in and looked at it. "Big foot," he said, looking at Maurice. "Real big foot." And she was a little mare. They pulled, she pushed. She got up and she lay down. The head was hard. "Pull, Maurice," Luther said. "He just winked at me." The chest was harder. "Come on, baby," Luther said to Wiggy. "You're getting it." The hips were impossible, it seemed. "We've got to rock him," Luther said. They grabbed the forelegs of the foal and swung them in half-circles. "Like twisting the cork out of a bottle," Luther said, grinning at Maurice. "You ought to be good at this." The foal thrashed, throwing them around. "Hold on, boy," Maurice told it. "You're about there." At last the mare gave a huge groan, and the whole thing came squirting out with a big rush.

Then there was all the navel-painting and cleaning up and

rubbing on the colt and talking to him and getting him up to nurse, which took forever because he was so big. At last they sat at the end of the stall full of clean new straw, one in each corner, while Wiggy took her ease at the other end, with her new colt beside her. Not yet grey or bay or brown, his soft, mysterious, undersea color, indefinable, silky, shining from within, his beautiful neck arched as he rested, nose on the ground. He had a great big white star, just like his mama did.

Luther had seen that star in a lot of winner's circle pictures. Wiggy had been a good race mare, but she hadn't become the broodmare he had meant for her to be. She'd had some nice horses for him, though—the best he'd bred, in fact. And he still believed in her, unlike some of the mares he'd kept. And last year, because she'd foaled so late, he'd gotten her to a better horse than he'd ever dreamed of being able to breed to. It was more money than he'd wanted to spend. But he knew that you've got to keep gambling, to keep your mind limber.

Still, he was always amazed by how much class his horses lost just in the process of growing up. When they were born, they were all Derby or Oaks winners. As weanlings, they won major stakes. When they were yearlings, it was just minor stakes. And when they went off to the races, he just hoped for a good solid $15,000 claimer.

But I guess that's the way it is with all of us, he thought. Look at Maurice—riding high at seventeen, then retiring early, as they say in the Form. Wanting to hang himself at forty-one. And here *he* was, himself. He'd made a little splash early, raised some nice horses, sold some high-priced yearlings. But the champions he'd known he was raising when he was young had somehow become just horses. He was still just a small breeder. He still mucked his own stalls and rubbed his own yearlings. And he still had his hand on every one of his horses, every day, and he knew by now that was what he did it for.

But he looked now at the foal in the straw before him, his quick breathing and perfect little head and the complex of bones that would round out into sweet, smooth horseflesh and carry him to his fate. And he saw that white star getting larger and larger, coming down the lane at him like the engine light on a fast freight train, while the others in the field rattled along, behind forever.

"He could be any kind," Maurice said, startling him, reading his thoughts. And then doing it again, speaking softly, kindly, almost laughing, "You was trying to kill me. Wasn't you?"

Luther grinned at Maurice. "For a minute there I thought I might have to," he said. "You can kill yourself all you want," he added, "but you ain't doing it in my foaling barn." He knew all that didn't make any sense. But Maurice nodded, as if he understood it perfectly. Luther rubbed his sore middle. "What did you hit me with, anyway?"

Maurice grinned back at him. "My head. I rammed you so hard I went over backward."

"That figures," Luther said, nodding. "I thought you was a goner. But you grabbed on to the rope, didn't you, when you went off? And then you climbed right back up it, like a bobcat on a leash." He shook his head. "I should've tied your hands back behind you, you know. Like they do in the cowboy movies. Do a job, do it right."

"Don't worry about it," Maurice said, quietly, drowsily, watching the foal. "It don't matter."

Luther groaned and pulled himself upright, ready at last to go home to bed. But he stood there a minute, listening to the meadowlarks outside singing their high, sweet songs, the sound reaching out to the edge of hearing and beyond, till it seemed to him, as he listened, that the whole world was just one great big green meadow full of racehorses, their silhouettes sliding along fluid and silent, their reverent long necks bowed to the

15

earth. He glanced over at Maurice, wondering if he could understand that, too.

But Maurice was asleep, his face looking softer and younger in the coming light, delivered from his nightmares into morning dreams, as they had both been delivered back into their innocence by the neat, smooth, strapping, velvet fellow they had just helped into the world. His mama was up now and eating around him in a circle, her nose turned always to him as if she were tethered. Around them, in the foaling barn, all the other mares were standing quiet in their stalls, looking out the windows at the rising sun.

# THE
# APE IN THE FACE

H e hadn't knocked. But Lydia unlocked the door anyway, since he'd been standing on the porch for so long, half-turned away, as if he weren't sure what to do.

"Oh Jesus," he said, as she slowly swung the heavy door open. And then, when his eye fell on her, "Thank God."

"Is something wrong?" she asked.

He laughed a little, shaking his head. "No. I just thought...nobody was here."

"You were right," she said. "In a way. The house doesn't open today."

He looked at her. He looked at the door.

"But of course, I've opened it, now." He blinked, standing still, not at all venturing to come in. He was tall and thin. His small neat wrists hung out of his sleeves; he seemed very young to her. "Would you like to see it?" she asked, at last.

"Oh," he said, as if he understood, suddenly. "No thank you. I'll just..." He started to turn away, turned halfway back, glanced at her again, from under his eyelashes. "Well," he said. "Maybe...if you don't mind..."

"It's quite all right," she said. "I'll be glad to take you through. I'm not doing anything right now."

She swung the door wide. He stepped carefully over the threshold, as if the huge house were a small boat, and might shift suddenly under his weight.

In the perfect order of the foyer he had a pleasantly rumpled look: rough red-blonde hair, too long to be in style; faded jeans; a white shirt with frayed cuffs; scuffed running shoes. His eyes were a pale, indefinite color, and seemed to gather the amber glow from the sidelights. He stared at her, for a moment, in silence. She felt as if she were being pulled, like the light, into his eyes.

She turned away, a bit dazzled. Still, she began as she always did: "If you'd been one of old Edward Clifton's neighbors, coming through the gate to visit him near the end of his life, he might have greeted you with a cannonball fired from his front porch."

She was used to groups of people, staring around her as she talked, at the paintings, the furniture, the walls with their mysteries of bloodstain or hidden doors. She wasn't used to just one person, watching her closely, as if she herself were the mystery. When she finished her circuit of the great hall and turned back to him, she was shocked to find him leaning against the wall, one hand splayed out on the handmade Chinese wallpaper. But she was also struck by the way he fit into the scene, his high-up gaze following her like the eyes of one of the portraits on the wall. And she didn't ask him, as she usually did ask people, not to touch anything.

Instead, she led the way into the family dining room in silence, and waited for him by the long table, which she'd just that morning set for the week with the eggshell-thin soup plates and the coin-silver spoons. He started toward her, suddenly went six or seven steps out of his way, then walked straight on to where she stood. He did this casually, barely glancing down, like a performer following chalk marks on a stage. But there were no marks here—nothing at all, in fact, to distinguish that stretch of floor he'd avoided from any other.

But she knew what was under this floor. An elaborate system of hot-water heating had at one point been built under it, with a boiler that was still down in the cellar, a huge shining brass and steel thing with intricate pipes and valves like a concert organ. She kept it polished, but had never fired it up, since the family had told her it always overheated the marble floor above it. "It would burn your feet right through your shoes," they said. She'd never thought exactly where the boiler was, under this room. But she could trace out its shape and its exact placement, as if on a floor plan, from the neat circle he'd made around it.

She turned to him, said quietly, "You've been here before, haven't you?"

He tilted his head, squinted his eyes a little, smiled. "How's that?"

She nodded her head at the place he'd circled.

He looked back at it thoughtfully. "Oh," he said. He grinned a wild grin, a great lot of teeth, rather mixed-up. He shook his head. "You mean it isn't—" he stretched the toe of his shoe back into the circle he'd avoided "—hot?" He nodded a little, then stepped back and stood in it, penitently, looking down at it and then up at her.

"It hasn't been hot since I've been here," she said.

"How long can that have been?" he asked, shutting his eyes, still not answering her question.

"Fourteen years," she said. She told him her name, nodding at him, rather formally. He was silent, nodding back at her. "And yourself?" she asked.

He turned and looked behind him, absurdly, as if there might be someone else to answer the question for him. Turned back. Gave her the mixed-up grin. Sighed. "All right," he said. "I'm Edward."

She stared at him, astonished. There had been generations of young men named Edward, including the original of this house. Just who was he claiming to be?

"You know. The one that got away. The prodigal son," he added, dryly.

She frowned. He had to mean by that the only son of the present owner of the house. The family rarely mentioned him, but she'd known of his existence, of course. She'd seen pictures of him, all teeth and eyes and legs, his hair skinned off, grinning hopelessly at the camera in his military school uniform. Soon after that he'd disappeared from the family albums. "But you're not—" not that old, she was about to say, before she stopped herself. That Edward was in fact just her age. She shook her head, embarrassed. "You look very young," she said.

"I *feel* very young, right now," he said, nodding at the floor.

"*I* feel very foolish. Showing a man his own house."

"It's not my house," he said quickly. He shook his head. "I can't tell you what a relief it was to see your face at the door."

"You mean...because I was a stranger?" She imagined herself as he must see her, so obviously foreign in this place, where the only represented human figure that resembled hers stood on the library mantel—a Sardinian statuette of a washerwoman, with her buxom body and her long straight nose, the whites of her glass eyes startling in her clay-colored face. Lydia had often thought that her own face could never have been one of the faces of this house.

"I didn't feel you were a stranger," he said. His voice was soft and full of breath, not at all like what she thought of as the Clifton family voice, which was a loud, outdoors sort of voice—

oratorical, almost shouting. "But I have been wondering about you," he added. "Have you always done...this?" He waved one arm around him.

"No," she said, wondering how she could explain her oddly divided life. "I was a singer, actually."

"Uh-*huh*," he said, as if that accounted for something. "What happened? You lose your voice?"

"No," she said, laughing. "No, I still sing, for myself. I still do my scales every day. I just gave up being a singer."

He raised his eyebrows. "That's a lot to give up."

"It wasn't, really. My father died when I was very young. My mother and I had to live, somehow. So I became one of those child-monsters—you know, the kind they stand up on the piano so you can see it sing. I love to sing. But I've always hated performing."

He nodded. "I can understand that. But how did you ever end up here?"

"My mother had just died. I was singing at the college. My hostess brought me out here, to entertain me, and they were looking for someone. Not someone like me, I'm sure— someone more traditional—a native, you might say. But I think in a way that's why they hired me. It was the unlikeliness of my sudden attachment."

"You fell in love, then? I'd think more of this place if someone like you could fall in love with it."

She smiled. "An ex-singer isn't good for much in the job market. I had no family, no friends except professional ones. I'd lived my life in hotels. But then—" she nodded, feeling the need to declare herself "—I did choose it, too. Or it chose me. I didn't want to leave. It felt like..." She paused, trying to think how to say it.

"Home?" he said, with a hollow laugh.

She shook her head. "Home" seemed too much to claim.

Still, here was the great house, rising around her: the carved sea serpents she'd uncovered on the old banisters; the fountains that still rose every summer at her command, bubbling up through blue copper pipes frosty with age; the ancient herb-beds in the courtyard that she'd restored according to old lists of seed purchases. "I'm like an old family retainer," she said, shrugging. "I feel connected to it, in that sad kind of foolish way."

"Not to my sister Pam, surely? With her 'Cliftonland, My Cliftonland?'"

She laughed, looking down. Pamela Clifton Bradshaw did want to sing, in her penetrating voice, an unfortunate song she had composed about the house, whenever Lydia got anywhere near the piano. "I have to admit, I need a little historical distance to feel that connection. The *first* Edward—"

"Ah. The patriarch." He was relaxing visibly, more animated, as he talked. "Another good-looking woman fallen into his clutches. Does that make you his fifth wife, or his sixth? I forget." She blushed, wondering if he could possibly know that by now some of the local tradespeople jokingly called her "Mrs. Clifton," as if she were married to the house. "He made us a lot of connections, all right," he went on, grinning at her. "Black and white, legitimate and illegitimate."

She shook her head in silence. She couldn't explain to him how the life of the first Edward, with its duels and scandals, its grand schemes and impossible coincidences, even the legendary rages of his old age, reminded her of the music she'd left behind—unequivocal, unaccountable, a maze of action from which the human soul emerged, mysterious, breaking the bounds of reality. "He was part of history," was all she said.

"Yeah, at least he's dead. It's the live ones you gotta watch out for. The family. They think they *own* you. They think they own everybody."

She put her head on one side, trying to be both honorable

and honest. "They've been very kind to me, and I'm grateful to them. They took me on, from the beginning."

She'd been taken on more, of course, when she was just off the tour. But she had, to this day, engagements with the Clifton family, which she always approached with mixed feelings of hope and dread. They were all handsome and sociable, and she was fond of them. But the truth was, she could never connect these present-day Cliftons with what she felt for this place. They all seemed to understand it differently than she did. Even the father of the house, with his upright military figure and his grand manner, finally wanted to talk about who everyone was, or had been. "Was she a Bledsoe? Or a Willoughby?" She was always grateful when they left her to the stillness of these rooms. Then silence filled up the house like clear water, and she moved through it as easily as if she were swimming, feeling her world shivering back into place.

"Tell me," he asked, "how do you stand all their questions?"

She had to laugh at that. "Oh, they don't ask so many," she said.

He grinned. "I *have* been asking a lot, haven't I?"

She shrugged. "I don't mind. They're all natural questions."

"Oh, they were always natural questions, as far as that goes. What do you think you're doing with your life? When are you going to settle down? Who're you going to marry?" Then he looked a little embarrassed. She supposed it had occurred to him that he had no reason to know whether she was married or not.

She was silent for a moment—not offended, just under-standing how long it had been since anyone had seriously asked her those questions. "There was some of that, at the beginning," she said, looking straight at him, smiling. "But by now, I believe, I'm regarded as a kind of vestal virgin."

He laughed, a sharp, admiring laugh. "I suppose that has its advantages, for an attractive woman living alone in this place."

She tilted her head back and forth, acknowledging, at least

to herself, both the advantages and the irony of those advantages. She wondered sometimes if this view of her weren't turning out to be the truth—if she hadn't, by her single-minded devotion to the house, purified herself beyond all other possibilities.

He studied her a moment, then came a step closer. "I'll tell you something, Lydia," he said, softly. "When you opened the front door to me—" he widened his eyes "—I couldn't see anyone at all."

She laughed ruefully. "You mean I'm disappearing into the place altogether?"

"No," he said. "It was me. I've been away so many years, you know. Today I had to come to town on business. I thought I'd just drive by. And there I was, suddenly, on the front porch. The door creaked open, the way it does in horror movies. I thought the house had just opened itself up, to take me back in. Back to that whole old life." He eyed the room uneasily. "Oh the long dinners I've eaten at that table. The hours I spent staring at the colors in this rug."

"Was it so bad?" she asked, disbelieving, almost pleading. "Really?"

He shrugged. "Well, we didn't break each other's necks, anyway. Like the first Edward did his brother's. But—"

"Oh—" she interrupted "—Edward didn't *mean* to kill his brother. They thought all those years that Julian had been killed by the Indians. So when Julian finally came back alive, Edward thought he was a ghost."

"So little Edward jumped off the porch roof to kill a ghost? You believe that old alibi?" He laughed shortly. "Julian was the *older* brother, you know. Everything was his, by rights. If Edward hadn't broken his neck, none of us would be here." She shook her head, disturbed by this view, which seemed to her colored by his disaffection from the family. "Anyway," he went on,

24

shrugging again, "he was whatever he was. Like you said, it's all just history now." He stared curiously at the room full of precious objects, each with its little card of identification in her own calligraphy. "I knew they'd sort of given this place over to the state. Something about taxes, I suppose."

"Yes. The family still holds it in trust. But it's a museum now," she said gently.

"Always was one," he said, flashing a grin at her. "But we didn't have you here. What do they call you? The keeper? We needed one, God knows."

She laughed. "The curator, actually."

"That's what *I* need—someone to cure me. You know, my dreams all still happen here," he said, his eyes moving from wall to wall, as if he were caught in some dream. "But from now on," he went on, nodding at her, "I'm going to put you in all my dreams. Reciting the family history to me in that sweet voice, as if you'd made it all up. Opening the door to me, with that perfect look on your face. Like you're not expecting *anything*."

"Oh, I haven't expected anything for years," she said, laughing, as they started up the grand staircase. But she heard the wistfulness in her laugh, and as he looked quickly at her from under his eyebrows, his pale gaze kindling, she wondered if what she'd said were true. Had she been expecting something, all these years? Was it Edward?

---

"The ape in the face," he muttered.

She turned to him, thinking she hadn't heard him right. They were in the room she always saved for last, the upstairs music room. It had, as always, its whiff of the world, from the silk curtains that used to be packed away each summer in cured tobacco leaves, to protect them from the insects. She kept the old canvas shades pulled across the back of the room, protecting the curtains from the sun, turning the room red in the waning light.

And there over the mantel was the portrait of the patriarch, the founder of the family. It was a face of great intelligence and distinction—the tall ruddy forehead with the white hair arching back from it, the shining direct gaze, long severe mouth, smooth gaunt cheeks. All the portrait spoke of strength of spirit, even wisdom. She frowned at it, then at the current Edward, confused by what he'd said.

"You've never seen it?" he asked, smiling.

"Seen what?"

"Come sit here by me," he said, going over to the piano. After a moment's hesitation she followed, sat down on the bench beside him. He stared at the painting. "I used to do this a lot. I had to practice the piano." He turned to her. "Don't you ever sit here?"

She nodded, smiling at him. "*I* practice here, too."

"Then you must have seen it."

She tilted her head, puzzled. "I've seen *him*," she said, nodding up at the gentleman on the wall.

"He watches you sing," he said, his head back, looking at her as if from a distance.

"I've thought, sometimes, he does. He looks very alert, doesn't he?"

He studied the portrait, his eyes narrowed. "Yeah," he said. "But something else is watching you here. You don't see it, or you don't know you see it, you just sort of feel it. Maybe it's there when you look down at the keys, and gone again when you look back up at him. Now look at him again, steadily. Do you see it?"

She stared obediently, smiling. Laughed, shaking her head. "Only what I always see. It does make me uneasy, sometimes— but only because it looks back at you so. It has that reality to it.

26

What is it I'm supposed to see? Something hidden in the portrait? Something behind him?"

"No, it's right there in his face. Most people don't see it, because they're not looking for it. But look again. His hair was red, originally, as you must know. Do you see a redheaded man—or creature—in the painting?"

She surveyed it again. She shook her head.

"It's the background," he said. "Backgrounds confuse people. Those carved lions, and that kind of pale sky in back of him, like a halo. But...you see how the white hair sort of goes off into the sky?" She nodded. "Now. Let the hair go, let it just drift off into the sky."

"All right." They were whispering, she realized, like two children at the back of a schoolroom.

"Now look down, just a little." She stared, her gaze flickering. Sitting close beside her on the bench, he turned toward her. One long hand moved down before her face, drawing her gaze downward; his other hand touched her lightly on the shoulder, positioning her slightly.

And she saw it, suddenly. The white hair of the man in the portrait disappeared into the white background, as if the top of his head had been cut off; the high red forehead was suddenly a low forehead, covered with close-growing red hair that reached right down to the pale eyebrows. The color came out about the mouth and brought the jaws forward, the nose turned upward, the lips thinned and turned inward—and a reddish creature, half-man, half-ape, its gaze pointed and cunning, gleamed out at her once from the face of the distinguished elderly gentleman. The lions rushed behind it in stiff poses, ready to pounce, the white sky burned out the top of his head.

"Oh," she gasped. Then laughed out loud, a shocked laugh. "Oh why did you show it to me?" she groaned, bending forward, covering her eyes with her hands. "Now I'll never be able to see *him* again." The two switched madly in her mind.

"Don't worry," he said drily. "He comes back on you. Still, the other one's in there." He smiled steadily, right into her eyes. His eyes were two colors, she saw, both blue and gold. "You ought to know it. I mean, here you are living with him, after all." She glanced at the portrait, then at him. She found herself blushing. "So. Do you ever sing for any *live* audiences in here?" he asked, in his hushed, intimate voice.

"I did once," she said, before she thought.

"I bet a lot of people came to hear you."

She shook her head, studying the piano keys. "Just your father, actually," she murmured.

He looked up, a gleam in his eye. She stared down; she hadn't really meant to mention it. She'd never known just how to think about it. "You sang for *him?*"

She nodded. "He asked me to."

He got up abruptly, moved a few steps away, glanced around at her ironically. "He's a very charming man, isn't he? People were forever telling me so. Was he the one who hired you?"

"Yes."

He nodded knowingly. "And when did this little musicale take place?"

"Oh . . . a long time ago, not long after I came here."

"He asked you to do it. So you did it, right?" She nodded again, hesitantly. He looked at her sharply. "Did you *want* to?"

She smiled, took a breath. "I could have sung forever, I suppose—if no one had ever watched me sing. A voice in the woods, you know," she added, laughing. She'd thought of that this morning, when she'd awakened with troops of warblers singing in her tiny backyard forest. She'd wished she could've been one of them, singing with her whole soul, invisible in the tops of trees. She laughed again, and heard her old music in

28

that laugh. She folded her hands before her, looked down at the piano keys. "It was...strange. Just the two of us in here."

It had seemed strange to her when Mr. Clifton had appeared at the door that evening, alone, holding his hat. But he'd said with a sigh, as he walked in, "I just felt like coming home." Touched by that, she'd kept him company, as he'd asked her to do, while he made his way through the house. He'd stopped last in this room, as was his habit. Then he made his request, bowing at her as if he were paying her a compliment.

And before she knew it, she was at the piano, sitting up straight, trying to please. The shades of past concerts around them, the pale water-colored programs she'd hung in little gilt frames on the walls, the wonderful resonant room, so easy to sing in—all lively humming wood, carved by some imported English craftsman in pineapples and pheasants and conch-shells, in this place that had never seen any of them.

But no visions of stiff polite gentlemen and whispering silken ladies on that occasion; just the one very solid man, his legs set out before him, silent, waiting against the light. The dark wings of the chair curved around him. After all her polite desperate demurrals and his playful, oratorical requests, *Now Lydia. I want you to do just this one thing for me*, the older Edward Clifton had said, his words separate, his loud voice lowered, soft and certain. He'd smiled and nodded, raising his eyebrows and widening his eyes at her, as if he were showing her a space in there big and dark enough to get lost in.

Still, how she had sung, in those circumstances, her voice released strangely from herself, separate, unearthly. *Sing like an angel*, her mother used to say, before every engagement. *Then Papa can hear you.* She'd never felt like an angel. She'd only felt alone. But she always knew when she'd done it—she could feel her dead father out there, listening, in the dark. She'd sung that way here, for Edward's father. He'd pressed her hand lingeringly before he left. And she'd felt, ever after, a faint uneasy stirring in his presence. She felt it again, as she looked up now and met Edward's eyes.

"That was all that happened," she said.

"It would be."

"He never asked me again."

"Didn't have to, did he?" He glanced at her, half-turned away, his face and neck dark red with anger or embarrassment. She was blushing too, all over, feeling her body suffused and revealed by his glance.

"He was lonely, I suppose," she stammered, raising one shoulder. "It was summer. Your mother and sisters were gone. It wasn't so much to ask."

"No?" He turned back to her, smiling, with that gleam in his eye. "All right. I'm the firstborn of this house. I'm lonely. And I'll probably never see you again. So sing for me." He threw himself down in the wing chair and grinned up at her. "Go on. Sing."

"Don't," she said, looking at him, stricken, seeing for the first time how very much she *hadn't* wanted to sing for his father.

"I'd like to kill him for you," he said, watching her, twisting in the chair. He laughed out loud, once, and jumped up. "And I'm jealous of the bastard, too," he said with another angry laugh. "That's the worst of it. I really do want you to sing for me. Right now. I want..."

He started toward her, his face blood-red, the gleam in his eye coming to a point. "Don't," she repeated, whispering, uncertain of him suddenly. "Please." She stood up, holding onto the piano.

He stopped, so abruptly that his body actually bent double. "Oh God," he breathed, as he straightened up. "I am so sorry," he said, looking very sorry indeed.

"It's all right," she said, speaking to herself as much as to him. He wasn't his father, after all.

"No it's not," he said flatly. "It's not all right at all." He stared around him. "I gotta get out of here," he said, in a low, amazed voice. "And I can hardly offer now to take you away from all this, can I?" he added ironically, waving one long arm around him as he retreated toward the door.

In the doorway he turned and looked back at her. His eyes were pulling in the light, as they'd done when he first looked at her in the foyer. She still felt the pull. "Thank you," he said quietly, "for letting me in today. Now I remember why I left."

She heard his footsteps hissing away from her down the staircase. A moment later, there was the sound of the front door opening and closing.

She sat back down at the piano, considered her possibilities, and made her choice. She studied the yellowed keys under her hands, then played a few bars, the measured convergence of chords that began Eurinda's aria from *La Doriclea*.

She paused and looked up. The ape seemed to have gone out the door with Edward. Only the patriarch looked back at her now, fixed in his place on the wall. Then she heard a click, as if the house had opened itself up again. Her heart pounded. She could feel her audience down there in the dim hall, waiting for her.

She played the chords again, musingly. The first long note of the aria was drawn from her, Eurinda's soft exclamation of wonder at her lover's unexpected return. She followed the flow of the music, phrases repeated ecstatically as if to make herself believe the unbelievable: hopeless longing fulfilled, love triumphant over worldly strife. Her voice sank away into tenderness, inviting her lover, offering him the haven of passion, free from the struggle and separation of the past. She was lost in the music, floating away from the earth with her voice, singing as if the dead could hear her.

She dropped her head as she finished, letting the last note

31

echo into the silence beyond. And felt a kind of opening all along her spine, as if she were being watched from behind. She turned around.

He hung perfectly still, his arms braced on either side of the doorway. From the depths of his eyes, something speechless and unknown was looking out at her. For all his disavowals, he was the true heir to this great house, the embodiment of its mystery.

She brought him in, holding his hand, as she'd wanted to do from the beginning, to lead him into his proper place. She took her time, stripping slowly, watching the strange dusky flower of her naked self emerge, exotic in the red-lit, opulent room. His eyes bright and playful, he sketched a little dance, shrugging, hesitating, arching his sleek body toward hers. She laughed and reached out, exposed his ruddy surprising length, that nudged itself up against her.

She drew him down, the soft worn nap of the Persian carpet shifting beneath them like an animal's skin. The white-haired gentleman watched from the wall above. Edward's face, a red mask, wavered over hers. A fierce grin. She smiled back, a helpless, welcoming smile. She closed her eyes. His bony weight fell hard on her. Still, he was apt, lucid, working at her and into her, smoothly, patiently—then smartly, impatiently—till he made her sing another aria, high and trilling and desperate, like a wild bird caught in the house.

Afterward, he propped himself up on one elbow, took in the music room, and her naked in the middle of it, with a glance that printed itself on her skin. An amused grunt: "*He* never heard you sing like *that.*" His long fingers stroked her knowingly, his light eyebrows disappeared upward, his many teeth jutted. And she saw the ape look out of his face— acquisitive, cunning, triumphant.

# CLARENCE CUMMINS

## AND THE

# SEMI-PERMANENT LOAN

C larence had a red, boyish face, turning loose around the neck now from so much looking around. He had a way of leaning back and surveying the world as if he were proud of it. He smiled a lot, shook his head a lot, and talked a lot in a high, mellow voice that tipped up all the time, like he couldn't believe anything he said. "Did you know? that when a baby horse is born? his legs are as long then? as they'll ever be?" he said once to James Petrie. He shook his head and laughed at the baby horses running in the field beside their mamas. James shook his head, too, but he never said a word. He was not about to argue with the best tobacco tenant he'd ever had.

Clarence's virtue was that he could never come on anyone doing anything but what he didn't lend them a hand. He raised three crops of tobacco on Bud Finnell's farm when James was running it. Every time he was on the farm, Clarence would lend James a hand. Fix a fence, fill a tank, put up or turn out, feed or hay—he would always stop and help out. James even had to jump in ahead of him sometimes to keep him from getting kicked or stomped, because he wanted to help do things with the horses he had no idea how to do. Still, James went around saying there had never been a tobacco tenant like Clarence. Then they asked James, one day up at the store, if it was true that Clarence was managing the farm and James was working for him. When James figured it out to be a serious question, he started laughing. "Where'd you hear that?" he said.

"Told us himself. Said you was a real nice feller, but he had to help you do 'bout everthing."

James dismissed any thought of mentioning that story to Clarence. What? he said to himself. And kill off the last case of noblesse oblige?

Clarence was going to raise the tobacco back in the field where James had his heifers. One day Clarence came out, in a hurry to get his beds fenced and seeded before it rained. After all, James thought, here he is running the farm, and I'm working for him, and so I guess he's letting me run those heifers back there out of the kindness of his heart, and then he has to go out and build his own fence just to keep them out.

So James offered to help, and under Clarence's direction they built a one-strand rusty barbed-wire fence with metal posts set down in the ground about an inch and a half deep, spaced out about thirty feet apart.

"You sure those heifers won't come through this fence?" James asked.

"They'll never even come near it," Clarence said.

They built a little more. The heifers came and stood around and watched. "This is an awful puny fence to keep forty heifers out," said James. "Don't you think we ought to make it two-strand, anyhow?"

Clarence looked around at the heifers, which had come up closer and were still watching. "Cute little boogers," he said.

"Nosir James, don't you worry about a thing. This old fence'll hold." He patted the corner post, and it staggered a little.

When they finished and stepped back inside the fence to look it over, James could hardly see it. A heifer stalked slowly up, staring at them; the barbed wire touched her on the chest and she stopped and looked down, mildly surprised. "See that?" said Clarence, nudging James and smiling. "See that?"

"I'm just afraid they might run through it before they even know it's there," James said. "What about if we tie some rags on the wire in those big stretches between the posts?"

Clarence looked around at each of the big stretches, smiling and shaking his head over the surprised heifer, and over James. "You know what?" He put his hand on James' shoulder. "I believe you're more worried about this fence than I am."

"Well, I'd hate for you to lose your beds," said James. That was all he said; it was as close as Clarence had ever come to reminding him that, after all, James just worked here.

Clarence kept on looking around at the fence and the heifers which ringed them now like the fence did, smiling like he was awfully pleased with the whole picture, patting James on the shoulder slow and careless. "Be all right," he said soothingly in his tipped-up voice. "Be all right. Don't you worry. This fence'll hold." James could have stepped out over it, but Clarence opened the gap for him, sweeping it back slowly like it was an iron gate in a granite wall. Clarence stayed and got his tobacco seeded before it rained.

The next morning when James went back to feed the heifers, two corner posts were pointing out and two were pointing in, and all four were lying in the mud. In one place the barbed wire had snapped and sprung to, like a broken banjo string, and there were little heifer prints all over the beds, and the whole seedbed had been turned up or dug under. Some places you could see the whole shape of a heifer, spelled out where she had

35

lain right down. Clarence came on the farm late that afternoon and drove back to the tobacco field. In a few minutes he came back, his old truck rattling hard as it lunged along, cutting a wake through the puddles. James went to the door and waited. Clarence got out of the car and came up the steps fast, shaking his head. For once he didn't look pleased. He just shook his head a long time, looking everywhere but at James. His red face got redder with every shake. At last he spoke, his voice tipping up now like people's voices do when they're about to cry. "I *told* you those heifers would get into those beds," he said. "I *told* you that fence would never hold."

So James was not really surprised when he heard about the pony cart. Clarence had been gone, out of this country. He had told James he was taking a job managing a horse farm down in Tennessee. James said uh-huh, and that he would miss him. A month later a man he didn't know called James up long distance and asked him about Clarence. "He's as pleasant a person as you'll ever meet," James said, "and he'll raise a good crop for you." He decided against mentioning heifer insurance.

"What about raising horses?"

"Horses," said James, beginning to wonder. "Well, he'll do what you tell him. But—" his conscience got the better of him "—I wouldn't leave him alone with a horse."

The man said it was already too late for that. Then he told James the whole story. He said he'd been running the farm himself, and since he'd hired this new manager he'd gone out to buy some more stock, and come back with a lot of wild Tennessee field horses, never seen a halter. Crazy enough that he just spooked the whole crew into jumping right up into a cattle truck, drove home and then spooked them into jumping right down again in the barn. Never needed a chute. He got them separated into stalls somehow and that afternoon Clarence

36

showed up to be the manager. He was on the trail of some other horses, so he left them with Clarence and went out looking again. He came back twenty days later and there the horses were, in the barn. Still in the barn, that is. What barn there was. Boards were broken out of the bottoms of stalls, slats were cracked in the tops, holes were dug in the stalls so deep it looked like someone was trying to tunnel out. Clarence had thrown in their feed and watered them with a hose through the slats, but he hadn't let a one of them out of the barn. He said it had rained all the time the owner was gone, and he didn't think the man would want them out tearing up his pastures so bad the way they do when it's wet. The man said they could tear up a barn pretty good, too, and the only reason he had that pasture was for horses to eat and run in. Had he not even walked them in the barn? The barn was shaking, hooves hitting wood like strings of firecrackers going off. No, Clarence said; the man said he had to shout over the racket. No, that would just make them wild.

When he tried to get Clarence to help him turn them out now, he said, Clarence just kept trying to talk him out of it. "You know what he said?" the man in Tennessee said. "He said, 'If I had a nice farm like this—' and he pointed kind of proud at the field where all that grass is so green and so deep from being rained on for three weeks and nothing eating it '—if this was *my* farm,' he said, 'I'd *never* let those horses out of the barn.'"

"That was Clarence all right," said James. "How in hell did you ever come to hire him in the first place?"

"That's what I called to ask you," the man said. "I hired him because he told me he managed your place for three years."

So Clarence came back to town. After a while James heard up at the store that he was living at the other end of town and digging graves at the cemetery. "I wonder," James said, "if he's letting folks bury anybody in them."

———

Then the telephone rang one night and it was Clarence. "Clarence Cummins," in fact. He announced his whole name, sounding so different from his normal self that James didn't believe it. No turned-up voice, just a kind of flat singsong, and lots of long silences, starting with right after he said his name. "Clarence? Are you there? Is that you?" James said.

"I never thought you'd do me this way," he said at last. "I thought you and me was friends."

"Do you what way? What are you talking about?"

Silence.

James was trying to think. "Are you there? Is that you? What's happened? What's the matter?"

"I never would have believed it of you," Clarence began again. "It's a terrible thing, when a man will go to all this trouble to tell lies about you."

"Now hold on," said James, bewildered but not mad. Clarence sounded too beat-down to get mad at. "What lies have I told about you?"

"Terrible lies. Saying I was—wasn't straight."

"Now, Clarence. I never said anything like that."

"You did too. I heard about it."

James had a thought. "You mean about that man from Tennessee calling me and asking about you and the horses?"

There was a long pause. "No." There was another long pause.

"Are you there, Clarence? Clarence? Then what in hell are you talking about?"

"You been down here telling lies about me."

"Down where?"

"Down here. At the store."

"You mean Rose's store? Up here?"

Silence. "No." More silence.

"What store, then?"

"You know what store. The store down here. Miz Bowles' place."

"Clarence." There was another silence, and James was figuring, making sure. "Clarence, you there? I have never been to Mrs. Bowles' store in my life. I don't even know where it is."

"You know damn well where it is." James blinked at the telephone. He thought about laughing, but he was afraid Clarence might cry. "You was down here yesterday afternoon, telling everbody lies."

"I was not down there yesterday afternoon. I was in Louisville all day yesterday, at the races. I had dinner and came back late. I wasn't even in town, you hear? You want me to get you three witnesses who'll testify to that?"

There was the longest silence of them all.

"It wasn't you?"

"It wasn't me. You sure it was anybody? You been drinking? You never used to be a drinking man."

"It wasn't you." Clarence seemed to be both cheerier and angrier. "Well, who was it, then? Who was the bastard? Where is he?"

"Clarence," said James, "if you're sure it really did happen—"

"Oh it happened all right." His voice began to tip up a little now. "It happened. Fifteen people told me about it already this morning. Everbody round here knows about it. It happened."

"Well, I don't know," said James. "But it wasn't me."

"Well, then—" Clarence sounded desperate suddenly. "Who *was* it?"

"Maybe if you could just tell me—" James started delicately "—something about what he said, then I might—"

"He said—" Clarence choked a little. "Well, I can't hardly tell you. He said I stole the pony cart. He said I *stole* it. That old

39

pony cart you give me out of the tobacco barn—you *give* it to me, didn't you?"

James was trying to figure. "Well, yes. I pretty much did. A semi-permanent loan is what I said. Anyway, you sure didn't steal it."

"See there? See there? And some bastard's been down here saying I stole it. Now what the hell kind of a bastard would come down here—"

But James had just had a thought. "You know what he looked like? You know what kind of car he was driving?"

"I was too mad to ask. But I am going to find out, you better believe it."

James hung up and sighed. It was true that he had given Clarence the pony cart. But it was Lacey Finnell's pony cart.

Lacey Finnell tyrannized the world by apologizing to it. "I'm really terribly sorry to bother you, but..." was the way she began every conversation. And the worst of it was that when Lacey apologized, she meant it. She really was terribly sorry to bother you. She was a big handsome woman with a girlish smile and a sweet penetrating twang and a nice soft laugh and an intermittent but persistent attachment to, or longing for, the things of her youth. And one of the things of her youth was the pony cart. She had driven in it around her father's farm when she was a girl, she had kept it all the time she was growing up, and she had moved it, when she married Bud Finnell, to the farm they bought, that James was now running for them. It had not been used in years, it was grey and covered with cobwebs and sat in the barn behind a lot of tobacco sticks.

Every spring Lacey got to mooning over the old pony cart. After she'd apologized to James for being there in her own barn, she would hang over the tobacco sticks and say, "It used to be such...the best times, just driving around with...the girls have never known...we could paint it up in..." And she and her daughters would have a halfhearted argument over what colors they would paint it up in. Over the course of several days, and as the spring wore on, the idea would drift away, vaguely, as most of Lacey's ideas did. To anybody's knowledge, she had never yet finished a sentence.

Now James had nothing against Lacey Finnell, or against her pony cart. What he had something against was ponies. "There is nothing in the world," he said, "so mean-spirited as a pony." When James came to run the Finnell's farm and put racehorses on it, it was stocked with a herd of foundered ponies. Nobody knew where they had come from, or why. Some of them had not had a hand on them, as far as anyone could remember, for six years. They stole the mares' feed, they could not be caught to be wormed, they couldn't be moved to rest the pastures.

One day James managed to lure them up into the trailer with feed, but there was one pony that wouldn't lure. So he got a rope on it, thinking he might pull it in. But when the rope tightened, the pony took off. James saw he couldn't hold it, so when the pony started off on one side of a walnut tree James ran on the other side of it. He spent the rest of the afternoon three feet away from the pony and five feet away from the trailer, with the rope bent around the tree and the pony on the other end of it, and James taking up slack, first hoping the pony would give up, and later praying it would strangle. But it had a regular pony neck, like a hippo's, and all it did was turn glassy-eyed and breathe louder and louder, and so did James, till Lacey heard them both all the way up at the house and came down to help. "I'm terribly sorry to..." she said, and jabbed the pony in the behind with a pitchfork. It was a masterful jab; it must have come from way back in her long-ago past of having to deal with ponies when they were bigger than she was. It was just hard enough to move him and not hard enough to make him bolt, and it had just enough stuff on it to send him back around the tree. All James had to do was get up off his behind and open the trailer gate and shut it again, and off the ponies went to the pony dealer.

But the next spring here were two more, only one of them foundered, the other blind in one eye. And then James began to understand where the ponies came from, and why. They came from wherever ponies always do come from when you have a farm and don't make a deliberate effort to keep them off it, and when they came they were destined for the imaginary pony-cart drives. When they had been there a couple of years and had rubbed their halters off on trees and let the children feed them and then bitten their fingers and never let anybody else get near them, and still hadn't pulled the cart, Lacey began to be disappointed in those particular ponies. So a couple of new ones would appear.

Now the grass in the pony field grew very high. James was going to use it for winter pasture, he said. By the end of the summer the grass would be higher than the ponies, but even if you went out and looked you wouldn't find one. Some got hit by lightning, some escaped, and some simply disappeared without a trace. Still, every spring, more ponies appeared to take their places.

So when, one day, Clarence pulled out the tobacco sticks, and the pony cart stood there before him, and he began walking up to it and smiling, and standing back and shaking his head, James did not hesitate. He told Lacey he needed the barn space just now, and he told Clarence it was a semi-permanent loan. And the next spring, when Lacey said, "I'm terribly sorry, but you know that old pony cart that was in the barn..." James said he was terribly sorry too, but Clarence had left the country, and he didn't know where the pony cart was. And the best of it was that it was true. Or it had been true.

———

The next morning Clarence called again. "It was a little skinny brown-haired feller driving a brand-new black Cadillac."

"Bud Finnell," said James. "I know. He just called me."

"Call you from home?"

"I'm not sure. Why?"

"I'm coming up to shoot him."

"But Clarence. It's his pony cart. His wife's pony cart."

"I know that. You give it to me, didn't you?"

"I said they got to take it back if they wanted. You remember that, don't you?"

"I remember that, and I would have been glad to give it. But you never told me they got to call me a cheap sneak thief that steals from women and children."

That phrase had made James' ear hurt when he had heard Bud Finnell use it about Clarence a few minutes before. Now it made both ears hurt. "All right," he said. "He never should have said that."

"Goddamn right, if he didn't want to get his head blown off. Is he usually home this time of the day?"

"Clarence," said James. "He claims you were trying to sell it."

"I never was."

"You know I told you they might want it back some day. Now why did you—"

"I never would have sold it, James."

"Well. But then how could you—"

"I got better things to do with that pony cart than sell it. I got—"

"Don't tell me. Please. Don't tell me. I believe you. Just tell me this, please. I know there has to be a reason. What was it doing there, all painted up shiny and new, and sitting out in front of that antique store?"

"Oh. I was just trying to help that old boy out."

"What old boy?"

43

"Well, I'll tell you. I like to stop in there, on the way to work, and James, that feller has some real nice stuff. Copper kettles, brass keys as big as your hand, things any man would be proud to own." James could see Clarence, leaning back and looking over the antique business, and, unfortunately, seeing something. "But you know, don't nobody ever buy nothing from him. And you know why not? Because don't nobody ever stop there. And you know why? Because can't nobody ever see a copper kettle when they're going down the pike at fifty miles an hour. So I thought of the pony cart. What do you think? Would that Bud Finnell be coming home for dinner?"

At last James got Clarence talked into not coming up and shooting Bud Finnell over his dinner. Then he said, "You know that old boy you were trying to help out? You know what he was doing? He was bragging to everybody that stopped about how this used to be Lacey Finnell's pony cart. Now I know you weren't trying to sell it, but I believe he was. And you know who he tried to sell it to yesterday morning? Lacey Finnell."

Of all the little back roads in the country, James said to himself, why would Lacey have picked out that one to be driving down, and why would she have gone right by that antique store, and why would she have—well, the rest was simple. There was a pony cart, all painted up and shiny. In fact, *the* pony cart. But it couldn't be. Still, she would have to stop and ask, just to be sure she was wrong. And then again, why did the antique-store man have to tell her it used to be Lacey Finnell's pony cart? It must have been some instinct drew her there. After all, it was spring.

And then, most of all, why hadn't Bud Finnell been off in Miami or Dallas or New York or one of those places he always had to be so urgently? Then Lacey would have just called James up and told him she was terribly sorry, and he would have found Clarence and got the pony cart for her. But Bud Finnell had been there, and had gone looking for Clarence at the store, and Bud was the last person needed to be messing with this kind of business.

Like a lot of self-made men, Bud Finnell thought that honesty was something you had to be able to afford, and as far as he was concerned, it came high. It was hard on him, always looking around and seeing all the people who didn't have millions of dollars, like he did, and thinking how untrustworthy they all had to be. It kept him stirred all the time. He was the only man James knew who would lock his car when he got out of it to talk in the middle of a forty-acre field, as if the cows and horses were going to break into the glove compartment and steal his sunglasses. Every time a strange car came on the farm, he imagined plots to kidnap his children. And he lived in fear, every day, that people were cheating him or trying to cheat him. James had almost quit him once when he came close to accusing James of cheating him over a twelve-dollar mailbox. And here, James knew, with this pony cart business, it was going to be hard to contain him.

There were no pony carts in Bud Finnell's past, and if there had been one, he would have sold it himself long ago. But that didn't mean he didn't value his wife's pony cart. In a way, that was why he had married her, not only because she had a pony cart, but because she wouldn't have sold it. It was true he wouldn't have valued it much when it sat in the barn taking up space and collecting cobwebs. But when he thought of it all painted up and sitting out in front of an antique store, and of the owner telling everybody it used to belong to Lacey Finnell— that reduced sentiment to negotiable terms, which were the terms that moved Bud most. Once Bud had given James' wife a puppy he'd bought and then decided was too much trouble, and when she had loved it and trained it and played with it and it turned into a handsome, well-behaved dog, he offered to buy it back for twice what he'd paid for it, and was surprised when she refused, and baffled when, after refusing, she walked away. Another time he had come into the barn when James' prize mare had just foaled. The mare was still down, dark with sweat and breathing hard. The little foal, still wet too, was just working to get up, thrashing and then teetering, then staggering and bouncing off the walls, and then standing. Bud watched it appraisingly as it wobbled there in front of him and then said to James, "What's it worth?"

"You're in luck," James told Bud when he called the next morning. "He's not going to come up here and shoot you. He's going to wait till you come down there."

"Well, James," Bud said, through his nose, as usual. He had been getting a cold all the time he was getting rich, and now he seemed to have a permanent cold, as if success had settled in his sinuses. "You know how that white trash is always talking. They're always going to do something to you, but they never actually get around to doing it. You scratch one of those rednecks and you'll find he's yellow underneath." He laughed at his own joke. "If you call their bluff, they're all tuck-tail-and-run."

James always had a hard time talking to Bud, because he hated to hear things like that, and when you talked to Bud it was impossible not to hear them. Usually he could walk away and examine a fence post or check out a hole in the ground till he got his mind clear of that kind of nastiness. But lying in bed talking on the phone, it was harder. Bud usually called him either after he'd gone to sleep, or before he woke up.

"You there?" Bud said. James was beginning to understand the function of pauses.

"Yes," he said at last. "Well, I still wouldn't go down there if I were you. It would be a damn stupid thing to get your head shot off over a pony cart."

"I'll call the Sheriff."

46

"You can't call the Sheriff. He hasn't shot you yet."

"He's stolen that pony cart."

"He has a plausible explanation for having it."

"Plausible my eye. Nobody but you would think it was plausible. In any court of law—"

"A court of law won't do you much good if you're exhibit A, the corpse."

"You mean you really think he'd—"

"On the subject of Clarence, it doesn't pay to think. He's a loose horse."

At last they agreed that Bud would not go down himself, but would send a crew down to pick up the pony cart. But they came back, the six men with the tractor and the wagon and the chains, and reported there was no pony cart at the antique store. It was gone.

"And before they got here I made the mistake of telling Lacey that little sneak thief was threatening to shoot me. And now you know what she wants me to do? She wants me to buy it back. And you know for how much? That antique dealer said Cummins told him he wouldn't take less than a thousand dollars for it. Now I can't do that. You know I can't do that. Pay some cheap sneak thief son of a bitch a thousand dollars just to give you back your own pony cart, and not shoot you. That's not just highway robbery, that must be blackmail. And it sure is extortion."

"Ah hell," said James, who had been up all night foaling a mare. "I better go get it myself."

The next morning Clarence called again, and said he was sorry he'd missed James. He went out to work in the evening and worked all night. People hated to see anybody out there digging graves in the daytime. James said he was sorry to have missed Clarence, too.

47

"Well, you come down and visit again sometime," said Clarence. "They told me at the store you was asking for me." "They told me what road you live on."

"That's a long old road, isn't it? You ever find the house?"

"Well," said James. "It is a long road, that's true. But yours is the only house on it that has a red and black pony cart chained and padlocked to an oak tree in the front yard."

"I'm not giving it back," said Clarence.

"You've got to give it back. It is not yours."

"I'm not giving it. Not till he takes it back."

"Now how is he—when you said you were going to—"

"Till he takes it all back, every word he said, he's not taking that pony cart back." What Clarence wanted, it appeared, was an apology. He wanted Bud to say he was sorry he had called him a sneak thief and all the other things. And he wanted it to be public; that is, he wanted him to come down and take it back in Mrs. Bowles' store.

"People who steal things don't go giving them back," he said. "If he thinks I stole it, why would I be so nice and give it back? He needs to get shot just to learn some good manners."

James said he'd often thought himself that was the only thing that would do it. "But why would a man come down there and apologize to somebody that's threatening to shoot him?"

"That's one reason right there," Clarence said.

Bud Finnell never apologized; he sent checks. And when he called James the next morning he was not in the mood to do either. "She's gone down there," he said urgently through his nose.

"Who's gone down where?"

"Lacey. She's gone down to get the pony cart back. I just got here and found the note. I'm going on down. You want to go with me?"

48

"What are you going down for?"

"If he was going to shoot me, what the hell do you think he'll do to Lacey?"

"He won't do anything to Lacey. She didn't call him any names in the store. Besides, Clarence isn't the sort who goes around shooting women."

"You didn't think he was the sort who went around stealing pony carts from women, either."

"I still don't," James said.

"I think I'll call the Sheriff and tell him what's going on."

"Bud. Nothing is going on."

"Are you coming, or not?"

"Well. If you're going, I guess I'm going, too. She won't need anybody to protect her, but you might."

Bud was silent on the way down, sniffing grimly, driving so fast on the back roads that his Cadillac rode the bumps like they were waves. James felt seasick, and a little depressed. Here he was riding down in Bud's Cadillac to find Clarence so he could shoot Bud over a pony cart. Now that made a little bit of sense. What didn't make any sense at all was that for killing Bud, Clarence was going to go to jail for thirty years. Maybe, James thought, it was his fault. Maybe he should have made Clarence sign an affidavit that he would never sell, try to sell, or let anybody else try to sell the pony cart, before he gave it to him on semi-permanent loan. Maybe, earlier, he should have made it clear that he was running the farm, and not Clarence. Maybe he should even have pointed it out to him that mares always have longer legs than their babies, and that Clarence was the one who thought the fence would hold.

When they got to Clarence's house, his truck was there, but nobody was at home. And the pony cart was gone. "He's escaping in it," Bud said.

"Escaping from what?"

"Whatever he's done to Lacey. Or maybe he's kidnapping her in it."

"That Dodge truck would be a lot faster."

Bud gave him a furious glare, and they headed for the store. There, parked in front of it, was Lacey's Cadillac, empty; and there was the pony cart, all red and black and shiny, and there was the smallest, furriest, grey burro in the world hitched up to it. And there in the cart was Clarence, sitting up very straight and holding the reins.

"You—" For once, Bud was so upset he couldn't think of anything to call anyone. "What have you done with my wife?"

Just then Lacey came out of the store, dressed like she was coming from a sorority tea, and carrying a big paper bag. "I'm terribly sorry," she said, walking up to Bud and putting the bag in his outstretched arms, "but would you mind just..." She started rummaging around in the bag while he held it.

"Lacey!" Bud was shouting at her over the bag. "Are you all right?"

"It's in here with the...Marge Farmer told me about this nice place where...the cutest little bonnets you ever... And so I thought I might find...but I'm afraid they're too big for the girls, and I wanted to see if...oh—" she looked over at the pony cart, and Clarence.

"He made you cash a check, didn't he?" Bud said, lowering his voice. "How much have you got in here?"

"There's almost...no, I got five, so I could..." Lacey then pulled out of the bag, one by one, five plastic Christmas wreaths and a red gingham poke bonnet. She put the bonnet on, and started taking the big red ribbon bows off the wreaths. "She said they can't give them away after...and she was so nice just to charge me for..."

"Lacey. What's the matter? What's he done to you? What have you done to her, you—"

"Isn't it just the cutest... and the little burro, he can... just exactly the colors I wanted..." Clarence was still sitting in the pony cart, very straight. He had never turned his head. A crowd was beginning to gather outside the store, lured by the pony cart and the black Cadillacs. And now the police car which pulled up. Two county patrolmen got out and walked over. "I'm terribly sorry to bother you," Lacey said, smiling at them and taking the last red ribbon off the last Christmas wreath, "but maybe one of you all wouldn't mind too much just driving my car back to the..." and she handed one of them her keys. "There now, we'll just..." She shook out the ribbons and walked over and tied them, one on each of the shafts, two on the back, and one on the burro's brow band. "If you just say 'Shake,'" she said, "he..." And the little burro picked up his foreleg and shook hands with her. She smiled up at Clarence, a delighted, girlish smile, and he smiled back.

And James knew exactly what had happened. Lacey had come down to the store and found Clarence here, where he would be, along with everybody else, on Saturday afternoon. She had held out her hand and said, with the smile that showed she really meant it, "I'm Lacey Finnell, and I'm really terribly sorry, but..." And Clarence had leaned back and looked at her, and at all the other people looking at and listening to her, and he'd shaken her hand, and gone to get her pony cart for her.

"Lacey," said Bud, "you're coming home with me right now, before this—"

"I'm terribly sorry, Buddy," she said, "but if you'll just..." And she put her hand out toward Bud's shoulder and gave him a shove, with a hard little twist to it, toward his car. She was as tall as he was, and a lot stouter, and when she shoved he headed right for the car door, bounced against it, and stayed there. "You're just lucky she didn't have a pitchfork," James told him.

Then Clarence got down and helped her up into the pony

51

cart, holding her fingertips and raising them way up high, like he was handing her into a royal coach, and he climbed up beside her. Lacey looked down from under the bonnet, at Bud, at the county patrol, at James, and at the people from Mrs. Bowles' store, who were all mesmerized. In that sweet, penetrating twang she pronounced her first entire sentence. "Mr. Cummins," she said, "is driving me home."

Afterward, James had the honor of hauling Clarence back, along with his burro. They rode along in silence, the spring air full of locust scent pouring in on them slowly, the locust blossoms littering the road before them. They came around a corner and there was the antique store. They passed it, and then after a while James said, "Clarence. Did you tell him he could sell it?"

The old, tipped-up voice: "No?"

They rode on a ways further, the trees bending in close to brush them with their blossoms.

"You told him he *couldn't* sell it?"

"Why no? I never told him that?" Clarence looked over at James, a mild, amazed glance. "Don't you know? That would have broke his spirit?"

# Man Walking

From time to time she saw him, coming toward the log house. In the field across the creek, coming down the hill, just visible as he moved beside the little fenced-off grove of old walnut and cedar trees, where poison ivy vines tangled above grey stones. At first she would think it was her husband, he would start into her mind with that glad start just as Will always did, whenever she saw him, unexpectedly, coming toward her. Thinking he had quit early; wanted to go on back. No, not thinking, none of that was thinking. Just the startle of it, without thinking, the pleasure. Then she wouldn't see him any more, and that wouldn't surprise her. She was always thinking she saw Will.

At last, though, after she had seen him several times and always in the same place and at about the same time of day, it came to her slowly that it was not Will she saw and then didn't see. It was a man taller, longer-legged, rounder-limbed; and his walk was different, slower, more deliberate. But purposeful, too. That was why she had thought it was Will, the intention in his movement, it came to her now—he moved as a man moved on his own place, heading home in the soft green afternoon light with its thick shadows. Coming for her, that was what she had felt, that intention toward her. But maybe only toward the place where she stood, in the log house, looking out the window by the fireplace. And she saw, in this collective kind of way, looking back at it and how it wasn't Will, that he was dressed in tan, not blue, as Will would be. And then last, last she saw, of course, where it was she always saw him. Coming around the corner, or out from behind the fence—no, she never saw that, she never saw him appear; he would just be walking along beside the fenced-off square of tangled poison ivy and old cedar and walnuts, the low grey shapes of the stones. The graveyard.

And all of it was comfortable, and known. His movement, his coming toward her, toward where she stood, back in the shadows of the log house. She saw him, and she had seen him.

When she and Will bought the farm, they had planned to burn down the old wrecked-looking house and use its handsome stone chimney to rebuild on. But then they lifted up the rotten grey-white clapboard siding and saw, underneath, behind the mouse and mud-dauber nests and the mud chinking that dribbled out, great logs sitting in there dark like a secret, some deep sheen of life still on them.

Then Will worked at the house with a wrecking bar, tearing off the old siding. He worked furiously, ecstatically, freeing the logs from their shell, shards of grey-white wood falling in chaos around him. Out of that chaos the log house grew up and sideways, taking shape from its corners like a jigsaw puzzle, the perfect proportions of its single statement revealing themselves again, like some old truth. Still true. One wall had bulged a little, where water had gotten in behind it, but the house stood straight at both ends and everywhere else. At last it was whole in the

54

sunlight, its solid lines against the sky again. Locust and catalpa leaves touched it, its wood ran once more to the living wood.

Hay had been stored inside, every inch of space inside was hay, as if the house had one day been drowned in an avalanche of hay, the fields coming up to shower down in it. They moved the hay out, tore out the old loft and interior walls, opening what had been four tiny rooms up into one great high room; they pulled off layers of wallpaper and plaster and linoleum, wire-brushed the logs, rechinked them. At last she stood, one bright late afternoon, on the bare new floor that she had just swept finally clean with a wet broom. She stood inside the low deep door, it fit her perfectly, its light a golden section around her. Light fell on the new floor, soft and diffuse, reaching all the way back in. It has always done that, this time of the day, she said to herself; leaf shadows always on the floor, shifting softly with the breeze. She saw how the logs rose around her, one on one on one; how everything rested on everything else.

She claimed the house. It would be her workroom till they moved out to live in it.

On rainy days there was an oddly familiar smell in the house. It came from underneath the floor, almost under her desk. Wet dog, it smelled like. Only very wet dog, the wettest dog she'd ever smelled. She had seen the old groundhog hole, obviously still in use, its little yellow clay trail going under the house on one side and then coming out again on the front side, with quite a heap of dirt built up there. On sunny days she would go, sometimes, and peer in it; if the flies stirred around the opening, The Groundhog Is In, she would say to herself. Once, looking out the back window, she saw a motion out there, almost saw it, only it was jumping a little, not running but hopping, skipping. A fast, jumpy groundhog, she said to herself. She could hear it come bumping in under the floor sometimes.

Then it was raising a litter under there, she heard little whining noises, like puppies, underneath.

One day there was a great lot of growling down below. Growling and growling, getting louder and louder. And a lot of thumps and bumps. Then suddenly the growling rolled outside, into the open, under the front window. A battle was going on out there. She went to the window silently and looked down. There, right under her nose, a flurry of motion, some furry thing, rolling and growling in the grass. The motion stopped suddenly, the furry thing divided itself in two: not a groundhog, but two furry fox kits, big-headed like half-grown tomcats, with large sharp reddish ears and little soft grey bodies. One was holding in his mouth the cause of the battle, a dead field mouse. He trotted back under the house with it, very proud, and his litter mate followed, dejected.

And then one cloudy afternoon the fawn came springing through a circle of leaves, astonishingly, as if it were leaping through a paper hoop at the circus. Lit, unsurprised, already eating, in the yard behind the house, its white tail flapping up and down. It was bright red, with large buff spots in a handsome pattern on its side. It stopped, scratched its side with a hind leg like a dog, stamped at flies. Grazed around, blowing thoughtfully. It was dim in the log house; the wind was blowing toward her, and she made no noise. The fawn stayed quite a long time, only stopping from its grazing more and more, looking more and more down at the house. Then it was gone, springing back through the circle of leaves, even more startling in its vanishing, as if it had leaped back into the sky.

When she got tired of working, she would lie down on the floor on a little pallet she had brought out. She would stare up through the great beams of the old loft they had torn out, up to the original ceiling: odd-shaped plates of old poplar bark that had been used for sheeting, held up by little trees that had been pointed end to end for support, notched together cleverly where they met at the top. The trees still had their bark on. Like living in a tree in the forest it is, she said to herself, wood all around you, rough and smooth, close-up and far-off. And lying there one afternoon, the still summer day around her, cool in the depths of the log house, she heard feet walking overhead, walking back and forth, not stepping carefully from one beam to the next but walking solidly on the loft floor that had once been there, the floor she and Will had torn out. She lay with her eyes open and studied the poplar sheeting and the little trees meeting at the rooftree and the open beams below, and heard the walking. There was not just one person; there were numbers of them, marching back and forth over her head. Heavy traffic, a whole crowd of people, noisy, rhythmic, but with all the footsteps jumbled together, bustling back and forth over her head with their shoes on.

The people upstairs, she came to think of them. She heard them often after that. Ghostly footsteps, she decided, were nothing to a real fox den under your floor, or a live fawn in your backyard.

But when Will proposed, one day, that they sleep out in the log house overnight, she hesitated. She had told him about the fawn and the foxes, of course; she had not told him about the other things she had heard and seen out there. "Don't you want to see what it's like?" he asked, grinning at her curiously.

She did want to, of course, though perhaps not in the same way he did.

So they brought their big mattress out and laid it on the floor. He held on to her, as he always did, right through the night. The mattress was hard on the hard floor, she lay awake while Will slept, with all the dark space of the house above her. But she saw only the moonlight moving slowly through the great beams, tracing the old axe-bites, and heard only the hounds running out in the dark, their desperate beautiful voices. She thought of the neat holes that hunters cut in the wire fences so their hounds could pass through. What was cut for the others, she wondered; why did they sometimes come, and sometimes not? What made them able or unable to pass through?

In the morning, with the logs glowing all around in the light as if they were alive, she told Will about how she had heard the people upstairs, and seen the man walking.

Will grinned at her as she told him. "How come *I* never heard them?" he said.

He propped himself up on one elbow and looked down at her quizzically. "And how come I never run into *him* when I'm moving around out here?" he went on. "What's he got against *me?*"

"Nothing," she said, smiling at him, shrugging. "I'm sure. He's...friendly." It seemed not quite the right word.

"Toward you, maybe," he said, lying back down, hugging her against him. "I'd be friendly toward you, too, if I was a ghost."

She laughed. But then she thought about it, staring up at the ceiling. "I guess you're not *there* for him," she said at last. "Just like he's not there for you. He has nothing to do with you, one way or the other. He's not friendly or unfriendly."

"Well, *I* might be unfriendly," Will said. "I'm not sure I'll like having all these folks around when we move in out here. Even if I *can't* see them." He nodded upward. "Does he tramp around up there with the rest of them?"

"Oh no," she said. "That's just your common run of house ghosts, up there. He's the *farm* ghost."

"*My* kind of ghost," he said, grinning at her again. "The outdoors type."

"That's right," she said, laughing, wanting out of it. "Anyhow," she went on after a moment, "it looks like you ran them all off last night. They'll probably be long gone by the time we move in."

She wasn't sure if that was true as she said it, or even if she wanted it to be true. But whatever they did from now on, she decided, she'd try to keep it to herself. She felt uncomfortable about having discussed them with Will—as if she'd betrayed a confidence.

She and Will had lived on one farm or another for years, but always it had been someone else's farm. Now at last they would be living on their own. But even after the excitement of all the plans, she was sad when she had to face giving up her log house to be made over into a real house. Will asked her if she wanted to build another house on the farm, a new house, so she could have the log house for her workroom forever.

"Oh no," she said, amazed that he would even think of it, offering her the very best place for herself. "I want us to live in here. It's too wonderful to keep to myself."

When they moved into the house, at the end of the summer, she did not hear the people upstairs any more, or see the man walking. The fox moved out. The fawn did not appear. But the farm was everything she had ever wanted—when they had first looked at it, it had brought the tears to her eyes. She had loved it when it was a tangle, abandoned, crazy fences and old machinery everywhere. Now under Will's hand it was turning into a beautiful farm again. He worked till dark every day, cleaning it up, taking fields back from woods. She found herself protesting as every poison-ivy-scrub hillside was cleared. But she had to admit that the meadows he had made were lovely things, she liked walking in them, their sweet opening up to the light, the shape of the land showing again. He was grooming the farm lovingly into what it had once been. And their life together there took on its own order and density.

Still, sometimes she found herself uneasy, restless. "Doesn't it ever scare you," she asked him once, "thinking that you've come to the place you're going to be in for the rest of your life?"

He shook his head, smiling at her.

"Think of it," she said, laughing a little. "We'll probably die here."

"I hope so," he said.

She stared at him; then nodded, wide-eyed. "So do I," she said.

One morning near the end of the fall there were the great white dashings of what looked like bird lime on the floor by the old chimney; she thought some big bird must have somehow gotten trapped inside the night before, some crow or owl. But all the doors and windows were shut, and there was no fluttering or rustling in the log house, and no dead feathered body either, like the dead swifts she would sometimes find inside the fire screen, looking painted to the stone hearth. She peered into all the dark corners for ruffled dark shapes or shining round eyes, and saw at last that other shape of life, the long irregular line of it. Again there was no body; but here the shed skin, stretched along the top log just under the eaves, right at the end of the room, as if its owner had dropped it there carelessly as he went out. Will walked out on the beams and reached it for her, leaning precariously, tugging at the tail; it clung to the log a moment, resisting.

It was not dry yet, still soft and elastic. She unfolded the accordion pleats of it where the head had come out, turned back inside itself like a sleeve shrugged off. It did not rustle, it was quiet in her hands. She measured it with her arms and nose, like a tailor making a fitting. "Just about right," she told Will. It was almost as long as she was. Papery but strong and flexible, Japanese-lanternlike, the strange stretchy expanding transparent scales of the belly, the handsome tighter frailer armor of the back. She examined it for its meaning, studying her reptile book: the anal plate was divided, the caudal scales were single. A nonpoisonous snake. She hung it at last on a peg in the new workroom Will had built for her behind the house, leaving it there to dry, when she meant to have it for a hatband. (Or in case you might need it again, she said, speaking to the snake, meaning no offense.) The smell of it filled her room for days, pervasive, strange, sweetish, not like any other smell. Snaky. And for months after that, even when the skin had dried and the smell seemed gone, a certain condensation of the air would bring it back again, so faint, so slowly coming, it worked its way gradually into her brain and was almost gone before she smelled it, like the memory of a smell, more suggestive than smell itself.

One early spring afternoon, smelling that smell again, she gave up working and wandered outside, walking across the creek and up the slope toward the graveyard. It looked like a miniature fenced-off forest as she approached it, a wild dark tangle in the midst of the now-smooth fields. It was the other way around once, she thought; this fence once held the forest out, keeping a little space for the dead in all its life. Groundhogs had burrowed on either side of the fence, moving in and out, comfortably, among the dead. She opened the little scrolled-iron gate and went in, walking among the monuments and headstones, reading the inscriptions. Old men and young boys, a lot of women of childbearing years, a great many infants. Little stone lambs softening into lumps, graveyard poetry improving as it grew indecipherable. The stones all seemed crowded up in one corner of the yard, as if they were leaving room, politely, for more. The other part of the graveyard was where the walnuts and cedars grew. Winter had cleared the poison ivy for her, so she wandered back into that part, where she had never been.

Then she felt them, underfoot. Field stones, rows and rows of them, each raising itself up just a little against her walking, just above the grass and periwinkle. Unmarked. She stood still, feeling how much stillness she stood on. The graveyard was absolutely full, she saw, they were packed in elbow to elbow— more than enough of them underground here to make all the racket she had heard overhead in the log house.

She bent down near one stone, not knowing what she did till she felt how gently her hand met chill dried grass.

That night she woke in the middle of the night, turned over, out of Will's embrace. And there he was. The man, not walking now, standing perfectly still, right by the side of the bed. He was so much there, so suddenly, that it seemed to her a violence, as if he had just broken down the door to get there. Will would wake up, she thought; and then what?

But the door was shut, Will slept on at her side, and the man continued to stand, a dark shape, upright and silent, by the bed. And slowly, strangely, she found herself sinking into sleep again, accepting his presence, closing her eyes and going back to sleep, sleeping and waking up and falling asleep again, feeling him still there, above her, his dark silent presence at last not fearful at all, oddly reassuring, familiar.

In the morning she wondered over it. The bedroom was up in the new part of the house, the addition they had built onto the log house. The man had come into a brand-new place, the part of the house Will had just finished making, full of their present life together. It was, she said to herself, an amazing feat. It was breaking all the rules. But then, she remembered, she had gone into the graveyard and laid her hand on an unknown grave. Had that been breaking the rules?

At any rate, she had been right in what she had felt in the beginning; it had never been the log house he was moving toward, those afternoons she had seen him walking. He had always been coming for her.

It was a late summer afternoon. Will was gone, off the farm. She finished her chores in the house and went to stand at the window by the fireplace and looked out just in time to see the man jump the creek. A great, forward, alive jump. He looked up to the house once, his eyes glinting gold in the last sun, one reaching look, as if he met her eyes through the glass. Then he came up head down, the way Will came up when he was on foot, climbing the steep path toward the house.

She went to a chair and sat down, waiting. The door stood open. But it's his house, she said to herself. And he would come in anyway. The shadows of leaves were on the floor, as they always had been, soft and diffuse. He ducked his head coming in, a practiced bow, habitual. He knew just how to do. He came straight to her. She had not moved.

"You all right?" he said. It was Will's voice.

For a moment she couldn't speak. "I'm sorry," she said at last. "I didn't know who it was."

He laughed. "Who'd you think it was?"

She leaned back and looked up at him. His shape against the light, looking bigger than usual. He was wearing those heavy khakis she'd bought him, she said to herself.

But that wasn't it. She would have to tell him.

"I saw you coming up the hill," she began, slowly. "And you seemed to be the ghost. You looked like him. You came from where he comes from." She still felt strange with him. "And not just that. The way you moved, your whole—atmosphere. You're *not* a ghost, are you?" A perfectly earnest question.

He laughed again. "Not that I know of." But he didn't come any closer, didn't touch her.

"You walked up," she said, trying to figure it out. "By the cemetery. Didn't you?"

He nodded. "I wanted to check the water for the mares. I've

got to go back over before dinner and turn them out." He was silent a minute. "So," he said. "Have you seen him all the way up here, then?" His voice sounded strange now.

"No," she said. "Oh—yes. In the house, you mean. Yes. I have seen him."

"In here?" He looked around him.

"No. It was up in the addition."

He was silent again. "Where in the addition?" he asked.

There was nothing but the bedroom and the bathroom up there. "Well," she said after a minute, laughing a little, "not in the bathroom."

"I see. And what does your husband think about this?" An odd comic voice.

"My husband's always asleep when he comes." She laughed again, uneasy, excited. "He doesn't do anything, you know," she said. "He's very well-behaved. He just stands there."

"You've seen him more than once, then?"

"Oh yes."

"And he just stands there. Where?"

"There. In the bedroom. I wake up and see him standing there."

"Isn't that a little—unnerving?"

"No, it's not," she said, groping to explain. "It's rather—comforting, actually. It's as if he were guarding me, sort of."

"Guarding you from what?"

"I don't know. Maybe the other ghosts."

"They don't come up there?"

"No, he's the only one."

"He won't let them?"

"I suppose not. Or perhaps they never think of it. They're very busy down here, tramping back and forth all night." She laughed again, nervously.

"That's right," he said, "I'd forgotten. The big square dance in the sky."

It made her uncomfortable to talk about it. "It is rather like that," she said. "Only not so orderly."

"He's the only orderly one."

"Yes. He's very orderly. Except for coming up there in the first place. We built that part, you know. So he shouldn't have come up there. But it was my fault, really,"

He nodded, thoughtful. "How was that?"

"I called him up. I didn't mean to. It was an accident. I put my hand on his grave."

He nodded again. "And he ... misunderstood your intentions?"

"Well, I'm not sure I had any intentions. I didn't know it was his grave, after all. But that night, bang. There he was. In the bedroom."

"Been there ever since?"

"Off and on."

"I want to see just where you see him," he said. He walked out of the log house and up the steps into the addition. After a moment she followed.

She stood in the bedroom door. "He stands right there," she said, pointing, polite. She felt shy of him, could hardly look at him.

"Come in, come in," he said, ushering her in, gallant. "Right—here," he said, standing there. "And you're right there." He pointed at the bed, her side.

"Yes," she said, staring down.

He leaned closer to her. His voice in her ear, thoughtful. "Well, how about it, lady?" he said. "Want to lay your ghost?"

"Certainly not," she said. "I like my ghost. I want to keep him."

"I'm afraid that won't be possible," he said grimly. "Lie down."

"No," she said.

"Lie down, now," he said, playful again. "This won't hurt a bit. I promise."

She lay down, looked up at him, uncertain. He was a black shape against the light.

"Close your eyes," he said. His voice sounded funny. She closed her eyes, smiling. But then nothing happened. He still didn't touch her. And she felt him rising cold and still as a spirit above her, cold and detached, a dark shape watching her.

Then a hand, very light, traced around her neck, down her throat, started unbuttoning her shirt. She shuddered. "You're warm," she said accusingly. Laughing, shuddering. "You're alive." She opened her eyes.

He leaned over her, the gold light in his eyes again. "Of course," he said, grinning at her. "Didn't you want me to be?"

But there was a strangeness in his hands as they moved over her, light as paper; and a strange heaviness in his body as he lay down upon her; and a strangeness in his open mouth, most of all. He kept it on hers the whole time, his face pressing against hers till she could feel the hard voracious skull underneath, always on hers, no taking it from her, as if her breath were his breath. She twisted, but could not free herself. And she could feel him still, she could feel him standing over her, standing over the bed, the dark still spirit, she felt it coming down over her again, the darkness, the sleep. Her mouth was stopped, the weight of the earth was on her. She opened her eyes and saw the limbs of trees blackening the light. The cemetery had grown up around them, spreading through the fences. There was a fox in it, and a fawn, and a snake. They lay together in the great grave of the world. She had known all along who he was.

When she woke she was alone. She could hear Will's truck, banging and bumping its way up the road from the barn. She got up and went down into the log house to see about dinner.

# THE
# SCREENED PORCH

The porch was the temple of the gods, where vines crawled up the screens like snakes and outdoors was a wonderful green blur. It was being inside the world. The bricks of the porch were powdered with the spores of the giant tree fern, the oldest sort of tree on earth; its brown living dust sifted over them, straight from the forest primeval.

And the second-oldest sister had seen a woman on the porch one night, through the glass doors, as she was locking up. Locking up the glass doors at night was frightening. They fought about who would do it. The lock made a funny sound, like a tongue clicking, and then the glass doors were staring at you, and as you walked away you felt something walking away behind you, into the dark, and you tried not to scream or run. It was hard not to scream, and harder not to run; these seemed to be their two main impulses—necessities—delights. The clutches in the small of the back, then the shrieks and giggles. The old house shook with their running, bare feet thudding on the Turkish carpets, and all the Peruvian pottery jumped up and down on the shelves above the library.

There were big wicker chairs on the porch, wing chairs with magazine racks woven into the arms, but everyone—everyone—sat on the long couch, all together, lined up, as if they were the audience at their own play. The cushions were old and soft and people tended to fall into each other—all distinctions blurred on the porch—looking out at the green blurred world. The lake was a blue glimpse in the daytime, and an erasure at night, the open dark behind the closure of the trees, and from there the great sounds of the frogs grew, honking and honking louder and louder as the night went on. In the garden thick vines roped from tree to tree, and the trees were full of epiphytes. The sisters called plants by names like epiphytes, as they had heard them called. Epiphyte, they said to each other, podocarpus, cocus plumosis, monstera deliciosa.

Here they were lined up now as they ever had been.

"Remember," the two younger sisters were asking the second-oldest, "remember how you used to make us sit on the gold couch and watch Uncle Jack till he took a drag on his cigarette?" A portrait of the uncle they meant hung over the fireplace in the living room. Its most noticeable feature was the cigarette that dangled from the long thin fingers of its subject. The second-oldest had always maintained that this portrait smoked, furtively, from time to time.

"And every time he got ready to do it," the second-oldest said, "every time—just at that moment—you'd both scream and throw yourselves face down on the brocade. So you never got to see him."

"Never. Never," they said.

"But he did do it," she went on. "And there would be just the faintest haze afterward, blue-grey, forming in front of his nostrils. You had to look hard, but it was there."

They were showing off, their silliness, their sisterliness, the peculiarity of their upbringing, like modest little savages, the virgins of this porch. After a certain point they had all rather raised themselves and each other, with small interference from the busy adults in their lives, who seemed anyway to think that worldly knowledge was mostly a matter of botanical names. Guided by the eclectic offerings of the family library, the sisters had learned etiquette from a book called *Perfect Behavior*, which included such matters as "A Correct Letter from a Young Lady to a Taxidermist Thanking Him for Having Stuffed Her Pet Alice." Recent history they learned from *Low on the War* (his cartoons of Germany as a storm trooper dragging off the young woman with "Czechoslovakia" written across her chest like a beauty queen), and anatomy from their grandfather's childhood encyclopedia, which showed little elves skipping through the digestive system. They all knew *What Your Handwriting Reveals*, and their view of sex came from *Peter Pauper's Limerick Book*. All more or less grown now, they were quaint girls, they were lively girls, and they were, above all, silly girls, inventively hysterical.

Each could do a good graceful swoon, blacking out slowly before her very own eyes. The oldest was best at this, having taken the title one day when, frustrated by their laughter at some minor sorrow, she had pitched headfirst down the stairway, the white bathrobe she had on billowing around her, and a wire coat hanger, which she had flung down, sliding in front of her, jingling like a cymbal on every step. Her sisters admired her high style, but they kept on laughing.

This oldest sister had periodically, when they were both very small, sent a playmate to report her death by rattlesnake to the second-oldest. A number of times the second-oldest had been led, in some anxiety, to the top of the hill above the house to view the corpse of her sister lying in the middle of the road. At last she had learned that a good vicious tickle in the ribs was the best cure for snakebite, and ever after she had a hard time believing in anyone's troubles.

The second-youngest sister was honorable and fainted only on the rare occasions when they went to church, and then she did it out of guilt, with complete conviction. The others couldn't help but feel the authenticity of the rifle-crack her head made when it hit the uncarpeted outside aisle on Easter morning.

The youngest sister was the pet of them all and the most hysterical, and it was hard to say if that was because she was fourteen years old, or if she would always be that way. She had been laughed at by the others when she was little for saying from time to time that she had a pain in her heart. They all felt rather badly later when it appeared that she did have a little heart murmur, but said to each other, "Surely that wouldn't make your heart hurt? Just a murmur, after all." They had been fully relieved on that score when the second-oldest discovered that she had a heart murmur, too, and, she reported, it didn't hurt a bit.

And now here was the second-oldest, come home with a man. A young man with a dark tan and a white grin, thin-faced and hungry-looking, sitting on the porch amongst all the fair, round-faced girls, with their foolish exclusive talk and memory and self-conscious reflectiveness. They all sat right next to him, taking him into the sisterhood, surrounding him with soft, girlish flesh, pressing against him.

The very first time the young man had come home with the second-oldest, the youngest sister (who was, of course, even younger then) had come and plumped herself right down on his lap. Later she confessed, solemnly and in confidence, that she had "dreamed" her sister had died in an automobile accident, so she could marry the young man herself. "But it didn't hurt you," she said, grinning anxiously, pleadingly. "It didn't hurt you at all."

"That's a comfort," the second-oldest said, grinning back.

That was the thing about being sisters. You told each other everything, even the awful things. They would have been awful indeed if you hadn't told them. The second-oldest didn't mind the "dream." Hadn't she simply erased the wife of her Classics professor often enough in her own imagination, without even considering euthanasia? But then, of course, she'd never met the woman; with a sister, you had some reason for tenderness.

But here was this peculiar circumstance. This young man had come back now as the second-oldest sister's husband. A young man in the family, on the porch, and on the couch, and one who would do—not a fool, as they all allowed the oldest sister's husband to be, but a clever one—one as silly, on occasion, as they were.

When they were growing up, they had all tried walking on water; it had seemed something they were always on the verge of learning how to do, just as they had all at last learned how to drop off into the lake, yodeling like Tarzan, from the highest arc of the bag swing. The youngest, one day this summer, had continued their old experiment, stepping off the dock flat-footed, with her sneakers on—it was, she had announced, simply a matter of maintaining surface tension—and had been called by him, ever after, Squashy Foot.

"Old Squashy Foot," he would say, nodding at her.

"Old Squashy Foot," her sisters would say, nodding at him.

"Cow!" Old Squashy Foot would say. But she said this on every occasion.

"Cow!" he would say. "The cry of the wild Squashy Foot!"

"Squash, squash, squash, squash," Old Squashy Foot would say, doing a jaunty, squashy little dance.

"Pardonnez-moi," he would sing, dancing back at her, "is that the Squashanooga Shoe-Shoe?" Then murmur at them sideways, one eyebrow up, "You don't mind if I speak in my native tongue?"

How could they mind? It was their native tongue. It was, in fact, as if a stranger had appeared in some isolated tribe and had, from the beginning, spoken the language.

And for all that he was marvelously strange. The younger sisters fingered his clothing, patted his hair, stared at him in wonder. It made him theirs, his being the husband of the second-oldest. Not more seriously than before, but permanently; they could keep him. It was hard to take the marriage seriously as a marriage—it seemed mostly an arrangement for their delight and convenience, the better to be silly with him. It seemed that way to the sister who had married him, too—that seemed to be the very best thing about it, to have this attractive strange man here in the scene of her dreamy childhood, all her old, lazy, longing days of ecstasy on the porch, quiet and alone, or laughing with her sisters.

She looked out into the dark and remembered the way they used to stand under the streetlight on pleasant evenings, puzzled by what they were looking for. There was something about that, standing under the streetlight. The dark all around, the lake behind them, beyond the trees, they stood in the yellow pool of light on the brick road that was still warm from the day's sun, waiting for a car to go by and see them standing there waiting. Restless, unsatisfying, very satisfactory as an activity for young summer evenings, doing nothing at all in the full view of whoever might come by. Few people did. It was not a traveled road. The palmetto bugs bombed down at them, so they screamed occasionally, when one got caught in their hair, and sometimes were altogether silent in the solemnity of their waiting.

She was still not sure that he was what she had been waiting for. It had seemed something vaster, more mysterious than any particular man. Still, here he was, and he was something in himself. And what a lovely time they were all having together. They had felt quite thinned out when the oldest sister had married and left, but now they were back in force, four-square again, as they always had been, and closer, in a way, than before, with her two sisters turning always to him—the youngest, in fact, clinging to him as if magnetized.

One night they went to the drive-in movie. The car was too small for them all to sit in the front seat, but the youngest sister couldn't bear the exile of the back for long and crawled up on the top of the front seat, as she often did on the couch at home, and lay there with her arms around the young man's neck. But the car seat was narrower than the couch, and at some exciting point in the first movie, she lost her balance and literally fell all over the young man, sliding off her perch and landing heavily, her hips hanging off one of his shoulders, her breasts over the other, legs and arms everywhere. "For God's sake!" the second-oldest said, not laughing for once. "Quit *bothering* him." That was enough to make the youngest subside into the back seat, in tears. The second-oldest had been surprised by her own outburst and was prepared not to be angry after that, but as the weeping went on, expansive, accusing, right through the double feature, she grew stony and silent. He cheered them all up on the way home by joking around with them, and everyone seemed to have forgotten about it by the time they reached the house. But once the young man and his bride were in bed, he reprimanded her, gently but seriously, for hurting her sister's feelings for no reason.

"I thought *you'd* mind," the second-oldest said, as her first defense.

"I can take care of myself," he said pointedly. "If I mind, I'll say so."

She thought about this. "Well, I'm sorry I was mean to her," she said then, truthfully. "But I wasn't all *that* mean," she added. She grinned a little in the dark, wondering what he would have thought of her the time she had, in a fit of pique, slung a ukulele at the second-youngest.

He was silent a moment, as if he were considering. "We ought to try to be nice to her," he said then, thoughtfully.

She turned her head slowly to stare at him in the dark. "As opposed to trying *not* to be?"

"I don't mean you," he said, hugging her persuasively. "I mean both of us. We ought to let her know we like her. Be nice to her," he said again. "I think she needs it," he added, in the little quizzical voice he used for making pronouncements.

She acquiesced, puzzled, but respectful of his sensibilities. She had never been deliberately cruel to her younger sisters; she had even, when she could, protected them from the depredations of the oldest, remembering herself what it was like to be younger. And she would, of course, have flung herself into any stormy sea to save them, if she had to. She had studied Advanced Lifesaving in school, in case some day she should have to, and in her dreams her sisters were always the ones she saved. But it had never occurred to her to be nice to them.

After that night, there was still a lot of silliness in the daytime, but they began to talk seriously about life, in the darkening porch, as the nights came on. Or the young man began to talk. He said that everyone was alone in the world, and you had to accept that. "But that's awful," the two younger sisters said indignantly. No, he said, it wasn't an awful thing to know; it was an exciting thing to know, and once you knew it you could live in the world alone and like it. But you were always ready to love someone, if someone worth loving came along. The two girls listened obediently, asking questions in hopeless little voices, with tears in their eyes, as if it were a lesson they despaired to

74

learn. And he responded to their tears; he told them these things over and over, tenderness quickening his voice.

The second-oldest watched and wondered. You might be alone in the world, she said to herself, but you certainly weren't alone on the couch. Here they all were, squashed up together as usual. So why had her sisters gotten so sad? They had always been so jolly, alone together. How they had danced at night in the tall, white living room, making their long shadows leap up together toward the high ceiling, like the Masai warriors they had seen in *King Solomon's Mines*. How they had played, banging on the dishpan and the rosewood spinet alike, making "modern music" for themselves. How they had sung, in what they called Chinese harmony, fifths sliding up and down parallel, turning "You Are My Sunshine" into some threatening exotic shrillness. If you were sad in those days, you got laughed at, or left alone. Or tickled, as if you were faking snakebite. How had her sprightly sisters turned into these sad ladies who sat around crying in the dark? Her husband went on talking, in his deep voice with its rich timbre, that in its lowest register actually vibrated the springs of the couch they sat on. And the youngest sister wept steadily, slowly, as he talked, tears sliding down her face, silver and visible in the dark.

What was she crying for? He knew a lot, but he didn't know that. He knew a lot about life. But he didn't know a thing about sisters.

The second-oldest recalled how, when she was even younger than her youngest sister was now, she had provoked her older sister's boyfriend to kiss her under a bed in a game of hide-and-seek, and then had skulked away silently into the dark. And she remembered how, when she was several years older than her youngest sister was now, she had danced a pure, pelvic rhumba with her older sister's date one night in a dark bar—all hips, no feet, as if she were dancing on a cake of ice, as her dancing teacher used to say. But the movements she was making they had never learned in dancing school. And when, back in the booth, alone with her for a moment, he had kissed her—his lips seeming to come out and touch hers without any of the rest of him moving, like the tongue of a snake—she had looked him right in the eye and said, "You got the wrong sister."

What had she wanted on those occasions? Not to seduce anyone, certainly—beyond the rhumba, seduction had been a mystery to her. No, she had wanted Safe Contact—to be kissed, to have the world put its mouth out and touch hers. That had been quite enough, a perfect little taste of the world, so safe and so dangerous—to be kissed by a man who was presumed to belong to your older sister. She hadn't even much liked those men. Of course, her older sister hadn't been married to them either, but what was marriage to a fourteen-year-old? Rather like a long date.

And it was clear that her youngest sister did like her husband very much; indeed, she liked him so much herself, this seemed only natural to her. She loved him, in fact; but she didn't need him. How much did you allow for need, among your sisters?

Because she had at last to understand, watching her sister weeping in the dark, that her husband might be right—that those tears might be coming from some real need. Perhaps, when the youngest was little and said that her heart hurt, it really did hurt. Perhaps her heart hurt now. Certainly she had some new seriousness in her tears—she cried quietly now, knowingly, as if suffused with all the sorrows of the world. And if she were indeed sinking into some sea of world sorrow, being snatched away by its riptides—why, the second-oldest couldn't leap in herself, she was no good at this sadness business. But here was her young husband, who seemed to have an unexpected knack for it, to be drawn to it, in fact—even to have the promise of salvation in him. An Advanced Lifesaver, indeed. His talent all wasted on her.

"But what if you don't find anybody ever?" the youngest would say to him falteringly. "What if there really *isn't* anybody?"

"Then you're all right anyway," he would say again. "It's more fun with someone, of course. But it's fun anyway."

"But you *have* someone," the youngest said back to him that one night. She got up from the couch and moved across to one of the chairs, looking from him to the second-oldest, her eyes flashing with tears.

"We don't know we'll *always* have each other," he said. "Nobody can know that."

"But how can you say *we'll* be all right?" the youngest went on. "How can you be all right if you're all alone?"

"You're not 'all alone,'" he said, imitating her sorrowful tone. "You're just—" he shrugged, smiled "—alone. It's not so bad."

"It's not worth it," the youngest said, shaking her head.

"What's not?"

"It's not worth it. If I'm all there is, for the rest of my life..."
She couldn't finish the sentence.

"You've got to be worth it," he said sharply. "You *are* all there is."

"It's not worth it," she said again. "I'll never be enough. How can I be enough if I'm not? I won't do it," she said, starting to cry again.

"Oh," he said, leaning forward suddenly, speaking to her softly, crooningly. "Oh. Wait. Listen. It's not true. I lied. You won't be alone."

She raised her head, hopeful, doubtful.

"Someone will always be with you."

She pulled her chin in, looking at him severely.

"The friend you always needed," he went on in that crooning voice. "The one you always wanted. The one you've been waiting for, all these years."

She looked at her sisters. They looked back, blankly. "You know who it is, of course," he said.

77

"Not God?" she said hopelessly.

"God?" he said. "God—I don't know about. But Squashy Foot is always with you."

Her head dropped. The tears started to slide out from under her lashes again.

"You know," he crooned tenderly, "Squashy Foot? The one that walks on water?"

She said nothing, looking up at him pitifully with her tear-stained face.

"Hey, Squashy Foot," he called, behind his hand. "How's your surface tension?"

She gave a little hiccup, halfway between a sob and a giggle. She widened her eyes, stared down at her lap. Very softly she said, "Cow."

"Uh huh," he said. "That's right. Cow. Cow is with you, too. Both of them. Call on them, any time. They'll come running. Here they come now." He started stamping his feet softly. "Squash, squash, squash, isn't that how they go? Squash, squash, squash, squash," he sang, on his feet now, stamping toward her, arms swinging, grin flashing. "Squash, squash—"

But she leapt up from her chair and flung herself on him, headlong, giggling. Saved. For the moment, saved. They embraced, turning together to the second-oldest, who was angled back in the corner of the couch, watching.

It is just possible, she said to herself, looking from one shining, triumphant face to the other, that he has got the wrong sister.

But his dark, gleaming gaze drew her in, beyond all ordinary lights, and she saw her sister's pleading, anxious grin. And she grinned back. Her sister was, after all, her sister. And he was, she told herself, loving enough, wise enough, man enough for all three of them.

Came the night when she wandered out to the porch a little late and found herself at the end of the line, with her two sisters already pressed close against him, one on each side. His arm was long enough to reach around her, too, but that didn't feel right. The second-youngest had become a wall of flesh, through which she must imagine her husband's warmth. But then that sister, being honorable, got up and said she was going to bed, nobly giving up her place.

The two of them beside her then, their familiar shapes growing strange, growing together in the dark. They sat for a long time in what she expected was soulful silence. The frogs screamed louder and louder outside, the screens fell away into the living tangle of the night, the porch stood open to the larger dark. And at last she recognized, in the stillness that had filled the air, the waiting her out, the willing her to be gone. What she was not sure of, here at the last minute, was just where it was coming from. From her sister? From him? He sat rather sunk down between them, an arm looped around each of them, his eyes half-closed.

She was not quite ready to submit to euthanasia yet; still, it seemed to her that the least she could do was go up to bed herself. Which she did, briefly, with no fuss, no "You coming?" The second-oldest had a sporting instinct. What she felt, as she walked away, was release, and a certain quickening of the blood.

But an hour went by, and the house stayed quiet, and sticky sheets settled slowly around her. The bright emptiness of the upstairs hall faced her. Outside, the facade of leaves, white and unearthly in the outside light. Some part of her stood out there in the dark, glimpsing smooth white limbs and strange dark twinings—in the cage of the porch below, her little sister and the dark stranger, enmeshed. She herself lay cold and sweating, all alone in the stuffy bedroom. Had she really believed she could save her sister by offering to share her husband? Over and over again she struggled to rise up, thinking to rescue—her sister? Or her husband? And what if neither of them wanted to be rescued? The thought of what she might find, down in the porch, went through her like a knife through her middle, pinning her to the bed.

Then the footsteps thudding through the house—all the things they had locked out in the dark, running back into it. No screaming this time; they were past the possibilities of screaming now. Just the noisy running, that heavy-footed adolescent gallop, through the living room, rounding the stairs. She leapt a little in the bed, feeling the clutch at her own back, as if those were her own footsteps, pounding up the stairs, running down the hall. A pale, familiar figure ducked past her door, so bent on its escape as to look almost headless.

So, she said to herself. It was as she had first expected. Just Safe Contact, after all. An embrace—perhaps a kiss—and that had been quite enough. The noisy publicity of her sister's retreat made that obvious.

But when, sometime later, she heard her husband's footsteps coming up the stairs, she was not nearly as relieved as she had expected to be. And when he came in the room and slipped into bed beside her—in the perfect silence that followed—she wished herself back in her old bed at the other end of the hall, with her sisters giggling and whispering in the next room.

Still, there was, perhaps, no giggling on this occasion. "Is she all right?" she finally had to ask. For she knew it was possible to be really frightened, even if all you had seen was yourself.

There was another silence. "If you want to know..." he began—but in such an unfamiliar, muffled, boyish voice. She had been so ready to believe in his male magic—as if he were her smoking uncle hanging on the wall downstairs—she had given all of them over to his supposed powers. Now she did want to know that her sister was all right—it was, she found to her surprise, the one thing in the world she really wanted to know. And she understood, from the sound of his voice, that he couldn't tell her.

"I'm the one that's not..." he began again. Not all right, that was what he meant; she could hear it in his faltering voice. She glanced over at him, softening. He lay flattened to his side of the big bed, reciting upward to the dark. She turned to him, feeling the expanse of sheet like a vast white distance between them.

Then he gave a sharp, startled laugh, looking over at her with a flash of certainty. His voice shot up high, cracking with amazement and rage: "She knew what she was doing," he said. "All along."

But the truth was, of course, none of them had known what they were doing. And she herself—who was, after all, the second-oldest—had known least of all. She shut her eyes and saw a pale, familiar, almost headless figure—someone who might have been her sister—running away from her forever, into the foliate dark. It wasn't his fault, she said to herself. She had chosen to marry him, and she did love him. Still, he had ruined everything.

# The
# Murderer, the Pony,
## and
# Miss Brown to You

Joel came around a curve on Sorter Ridge, hauling a mare to the breeding shed, and found the local murderer trying to choke a pony. The pony was lying in the middle of the road, with two ropes in slipknots around its neck. The murderer and one of his sons were laying back on the ropes, and the other two sons were beating the pony with cedar trees.

Joel wasn't really surprised. Today was the vernal equinox, after all, a good old day for strange, primitive rites. And Sorter Ridge was the logical place for such doings. It was the outlaw edge of two counties, home to deer-spotters and chicken-fighters, and people rumored to deal marijuana out of hollow trees.

And the mare in the trailer was his prize broodmare, Soft Spot. That was the real reason he wasn't surprised.

He stopped the truck and opened the trailer door to check on her, and there she was, looking the way she always did in the trailer—bug-eyed, sweating, shaking violently, as if she expected to be at least mutilated. "You'll be all right," Joel told her, patting her. But he wasn't so sure about this pony. "Don't look," he advised her, closing the shutter, so she couldn't.

Joel had never seen the murderer in person—the man was a recluse. But his sons were grown men, though they still lived with their father, and they sometimes came to town. And the murderer's picture had been all over the newspapers a year ago. It wasn't a face you forget—white skin, long black hair, hacked-out features, fanatical eyes. He'd killed a deer hunter who'd ventured onto his farm. The murderer claimed he'd shot in self-defense, after the hunter aimed a rifle at him. But the hunter had been found with his rifle by his right hand, and a cigarette still clutched between the fingers of his left. And his name was Lefty. Still, the hunter had been trespassing, so they'd turned the murderer loose. Now here he was, blocking the road, doing his best to murder this little spotted pony. He had his rope so tight around the pony's neck that blood was coming out of its nose, and you couldn't get your finger between the rope and the neck. Joel knew, because he tried.

First he asked them if the pony was hurt, if that was how it got down.

"Naw, it ain't hurt," the murderer said indignantly. "It's wild. It'd run right off if we didn't have the ropes on it."

Since the pony was lying flat on its side, all broken out in a sweat, with its breath gurgling in and out, Joel wasn't sure that this was true. He went and got his spare halter out of the truck.

Once you own a racehorse, you never know where or when you're going to meet it running loose around the country, with no halter on. Your mind is full of racehorses—running down roads, through woods, across yards—all without halters. You see them coming at you from every direction. So you always keep a spare halter in your truck, in hopes of capturing some loose horse with it. And Joel made doubly sure he had a spare halter when he was hauling Soft Spot.

Because Soft Spot had a history of escaping from trailers. On her very first trailer ride, she'd thrown a fit, busted her halter, kicked the tailgate till she bent the five-eighths-inch steel latches, and jumped out, just as Joel managed to stop, in the middle of rush hour on Russell Cave Road. Horses have the right-of-way in this country, so traffic stopped, and people got out of their cars to help Joel catch her and put her back in the trailer and wire the tailgate shut.

After that, he had the latches replaced with two-inch steel. Still, on the way to a race, she kicked down the tailgate again, got loose on the Interstate, ran across three lanes of traffic, and started down the median toward home. She was out of sight by the time he got across the three lanes, but he ran after her, yelling desperately and idiotically, "Softy!" Miraculously, her sweet high whinny came in answer. She galloped back to him, got in the trailer, and made it to Churchill in time to run second in a stakes race.

Now she was stamping and sweating in the trailer here on Sorter Ridge Road, while Joel tried to put his spare halter on a murderer's pony. And the murderer was objecting to having his own ropes taken off his own pony by someone he didn't even know, figuring his pony was already long gone, now that it wasn't actually strangling any more.

But it didn't look to Joel as if this pony would go anywhere. It was lying there in perfect dignity, apparently prepared to die on the vernal equinox, a sacrificial victim in the name of warm winters or wet summers perhaps—who knew what the murderer might have in mind?

Or did he have anything in mind at all? Was his presence here just part of the machinations of Soft Spot's mama, that wily old witch-mare, Miss Brown?

Joel had met Miss Brown when he was first learning the horse business, working as a groom on the old Snyder farm. Her full name was Miss Brown to You. She was then eleven years old, and she'd had only one foal in her life. But that foal was a filly who became Broodmare of the Year, having had nine straight stakes winners of the Derby-Belmont-St. Leger variety.

Miss Brown was a squat, mule-eared, chocolate-colored mare with bulging eyes that were yellow around the outside, accurately representing her jaundiced attitude. When you went to catch her in the field, she'd walk away from you, fast and steady. If you tried to corner her, she'd run over you or through you. When at last she did let you catch her, she'd drag you to the barn, practically knock you down to get into the stall first, then swing her head around and give you a disgusted look, as if that was where she'd wanted to go all the time. It was at this point that you most wanted to kill her.

But once you got her in the stall, it seemed more likely she would kill you. She watched you all the time, her eye turned back in a baleful glare. If you stood on her left side, she'd pick up her left hind foot and hold it cocked. If you moved around to her right, she'd pick up her right hind.

She had everybody on the Snyder farm buffaloed—especially the teaser. Joel had watched many times as the spotted pony stud they used as a teaser was led through the barn to inquire of the mares, bravely and hopefully, whether each one might be "In" (heat, that is) on that particular day. "Some days they like you, and some days they don't," the teaser man would explain to the teaser. "But *she* ain't never liked you," he'd add, as Miss Brown roared and backed up, kicking the stall door, the walls, and the teaser. Miss Brown, the pony always reported, rolling his eyes, was "Out."

Still, Joel had watched her in the field, and he noticed

occasions on which Miss Brown was almost sociable, for her. That is, she didn't threaten the life of every creature that came near her. On those occasions, Joel suspected, the devious Miss Brown was "In." He thought she'd figured out that the pony was there just to tease her into admitting her vulnerable hormonal state. Joel explained this theory to the people in charge at Snyder's. But he was a lowly groom, new to the business, and they weren't about to take Miss Brown to the breeding shed and let her tear up some high-priced stud on his say-so.

At last the Snyders gave up on Miss Brown and sold her. She went for $2,000. By that time, Joel had his own little breeding operation in the Outer Bluegrass. He was the only one who bid on her. A friend agreed to breed her to his so-so stallion without teasing her, on what Joel judged to be one of her mellow days. There in the breeding shed was Miss Brown, looking evil as ever. The horse was brought in. He wasn't a great horse, but he was a thoroughbred stallion, not a pony teaser. As Joel had suspected, Miss Brown knew the difference. She stood for him.

The day Miss Brown was to be examined for pregnancy, it took fifty minutes—a new track record—to catch her in the field. Joel's friend the veterinarian, who knew Miss Brown well, said as he waited, "If you ever do catch her, and she's not in foal, let's cut her throat."

Miss Brown didn't get her throat cut. It took her twelve months, instead of the usual eleven months plus; still, at the age of nineteen, she had her second foal, a brown filly built like her, but with little ears and a wide-eyed, innocent face. On his rocky rail-fenced farm, Joel had a filly who was a half-sister to a Broodmare of the Year. He was ecstatic.

And Miss Brown loved her baby. The other mares weren't allowed to even look at her foal. If the foal strayed off to play with the other babies, Miss Brown would call her back. She had a deep, husky, authoritative bellow, like a horse blues-singer.

Several times a day, Joel would hear that distinctive call, then the foal's sweet high reply, and see her racing back obediently to her mama's side.

Every morning, Miss Brown took her daughter out and taught her how to run. Joel watched the tiny brown filly shadowing the little brown mare as they turned big counterclockwise circles around the field. Both of them ran like hound-dogs, their heads down low, with a flat, noiseless, stretched-out stride that seemed unlikely on such high-butted sprinter types. Joel named the filly Soft Spot; she was the one soft spot he'd found in Miss Brown's fierce heart.

Soft Spot was what people out here called "real pettified," as sweet and friendly as her mother was shrewd and suspicious. Like a lot of overprotected children, she grew up to be sensitive, a worrier, always a little bewildered, as if she were still expecting her mother to tell her what to do.

Joel trained her himself, at the local tracks. She won six races and some decent stakes, and last fall Joel had brought her home to replace her mother in his broodmare band.

Because after Joel solved her teaser problem, Miss Brown managed to develop an exotic infection which kept her from getting pregnant. She was, anyway, twenty-two years old. So Joel and his wife had officially retired her—trailered her up to their cattle farm and turned her out. They took off her halter and watched as she galloped away, hollering and tossing her head as if she'd been waiting all her life for this moment. Joel's wife got tears in her eyes, and sang "Turn My Horses Free."

After that, nobody tried to catch Miss Brown any more. She had her own house, an abandoned cabin that she haunted, lurking in its shadows along with owls and bats. But when Joel's wife had gone up to leave feed for her recently, she came back saying she thought Miss Brown was depressed. "She doesn't eat.

She hardly even comes out to graze any more. Maybe she's lonely," she added, giving Joel a significant look.

"Oh no," Joel said. "We're not bringing her back here. No no no," he repeated, to himself as much as to his wife. He too was uneasy with the image of Miss Brown alone in her dark house, peering out from under the doorway, her forelock full of cockleburs. And he sort of missed having her drag him to the barn every day, knocking him sideways, giving him sarcastic looks.

Still, there was Soft Spot. Soft Spot didn't have her mother's prejudice against teasers. In fact, she showed "In" enthusiastically, to everyone and everything—the teaser, the other mares, Joel, stray dogs and cats. Joel had every hope of getting lots of foals out of Soft Spot. Miss Brown had taught her daughter to run, it was true. But he couldn't have her giving Soft Spot advice on her new career, lest she also limit her production to one foal per decade. "I don't want her anywhere near Soft Spot," he said.

But she was near Soft Spot now. Around the next curve, here on Sorter Ridge Road, was Joel's cattle farm—Miss Brown's abode.

He hadn't wanted to bring Soft Spot this way. He'd been surprised, in fact, at how much he hadn't wanted to. But a flash flood had blocked the other road. And after all, he'd asked himself, what can Miss Brown do? Lay a hex on her through the trailer window as we drive by? Leap over the fence and throw herself down in front of the truck to stop us?

Now, on her first trip to the breeding shed, with a perfect, large, very soft follicle on her left ovary, Soft Spot had been stopped, in what was undoubtedly Miss Brown's force-field, by this murderer and his pony. Joel nodded grimly, patting the pony as he took off the ropes.

The pony didn't seem to care much. Joel could understand its depression. If it did get up, after all, it had to go home with the murderer—he owned it. "I been hunting it all over," he kept muttering.

At last Joel got the halter on. The ropes were loose, looped around the pony's neck. He patted it till it relaxed—its legs drooped down, instead of sticking straight out like a china pony knocked over on somebody's mantel, and its head sank toward the ground. Joel folded its feet under it, and rolled it up on its sternum. The murderer and his sons glanced at each other warningly; clearly, a sitting-up pony was the next thing to a running-off pony. Joel walked up to the truck to get his whip, which is the other thing horse people carry with them all the time, to load up all the loose horses in their mind, although you have to know which horses to use it on.

Take, for example, Soft Spot. She'd never seemed to mind the whip when she was running, but she'd become very sensitive to it when it was associated with loading into trailers. She was so sensitive by now that if you even touched her with a whip anywhere near a trailer, she'd try to kill you with her hind feet. You whipped, she kicked. Instantly. Every time. A big snapper kick, one of those where you could hear her joints pop.

So this morning Joel had explored alternative horse-loading methods. He'd tried chucking pieces of gravel at her. He'd tried a broom. He'd tried feed, and a blindfold. Nothing worked. What worked, finally, was desperation—he put his arms around her neck and begged her to go in the trailer, telling her sincerely that he loved her, that he'd never asked her to do anything dangerous, and he wasn't this time either. Of course, he hadn't considered the possibility of murderers and ponies.

"Hold on," he said to Soft Spot now. People are always saying to their horses what they need to hear themselves.

He got his whip out of the truck, a little whip like a spinning rod. He cut the pony with it lightly, and the pony stood up.

And the murderer and his sons laid back on the ropes again,

yelling at each other, "Look out! There it goes! It's going!" And the pony fell back down on the road.

Joel went through it all again, got the pony sitting up, got it to relax. "Now don't pull back when it gets up," he told them.

"Oh, it'll be gone," said the murderer. But his sons agreed not to, and this time one of the sons actually helped get the ropes loose. The pony got up again. It stood with its head hanging down, upright but fixed, never going to move again, this pony. Been cast in bronze in the middle of the road—a monument to the inhumanity of man to ponies. They had some corn in a plastic cup they'd used to catch it in the first place, so Joel held the cup out in front of it, to get it to take a step. But it stared at the ground and wouldn't move.

Now, Joel knew this was serious. A pony that won't take a step to get a bite of feed—this is a deeply troubled pony. A pony that won't eat is a pony that has given up, and is on its way to the big pony farm in the sky. At last Joel took a handful of the corn and held it right on the pony's nose, where the pony had to smell it. Very delicately, the pony took one grain out of his hand, then two. It didn't take a big sniff and inhale all the corn, like a regular pony would do. Still, this was progress.

He stood away from it and offered it the cup, and the pony took a step. The murderer and his sons were poised, ready to haul back on their ropes and stop the rogue pony from dashing into the bushes. Joel patted it on the withers and the rump, and it began to walk, slowly, beside him. It was six years old, they'd told him, and it had never been broken to lead. It was a mystery what they wanted it for, in that case. But they'd obviously been willing to kill it to get it back.

They had three miles to go to reach home. Joel cut a length of rope for a makeshift lead shank, gave one of the sons his whip and said, "But don't hit it. If it slows down, just shake the whip at it." He could only hope they'd follow instructions better than some jockeys he'd had.

He started out with them, leading the pony over the top of the hill behind the trailer. Then he handed the rope shank to the son that had helped him with the ropes, asking that they put his halter and whip back by his mailbox sometime.

"If it stops, don't haul on it," he said. "It's sulking, so you have to back off. Just pat it here and here," showing them, "and I think it'll go with you all the way."

The murderer said, by way of thanking him, Joel supposed, "I knew a cow would sulk. But I didn't know a horse would."

Joel watched till they got over the top of the next hill—the little spotted pony, the four big men. The pony went along sedately between them. The murderer was now carrying the whip, Joel noted, and they were all watching the pony warily, but they were doing what he'd said. The wife of one of them had been sitting up the road waiting for them, in a vast, ancient Buick. It shook into life, loosing a cloud of exhaust, and chugged off at a stately pace to follow them home. Joel turned and started jogging back to his truck.

When he neared the top of the hill above the trailer, there was a sound like a rifle shot. He froze, feeling sick. Then there was another sound, the same kind, and he realized the sounds weren't coming from behind him, the direction of the pony. They were coming from ahead of him—the direction of Soft Spot.

As he raced over the hill, there was another bang, and he saw the tailgate of his trailer bulge. The bangs came faster and louder, like a frenzied drum solo. At last there was one huge double bang. The tailgate heaved twice, looking oddly fluid, and flopped open, and Soft Spot came slithering backward out of the trailer, squatting down, her busted halter dangling horseless from the tie-strap, and her eyes wild, as if she were being attacked by demons.

92

Joel moved toward her quickly and quietly. But she started away from him, up the road. On the one hand, she was running the opposite way from the murderer and the pony. On the other hand, she was running toward his cattle farm—Miss Brown's territory. "Softy!" he yelled, as desperately as he'd done that day on the Interstate.

And he heard, in reply, a faint, shrill, mournful whinny. But not from Soft Spot. The sound came from behind him. The pony had answered him.

Soft Spot had heard it, too. She came running back. She'd recovered her sweet-young-thing look, and went bouncing past him with her ears pricked, heading straight for the murderer and the pony.

What would the murderer do, Joel asked himself as he ran after her, at this new threat to his reclaimed pony? Did he have a gun stashed in the Buick that was following them? When Soft Spot came barreling over the hill like the marauding wild horse the murderer obviously thought all horses to be, would he shoot her and claim self-defense of pony?

As Joel got to the top of the next hill, Soft Spot was bearing down on them. There was a great shout in front of him, white faces turning. The sons scattered. The murderer stood his ground and raised the whip. Soft Spot spun. The murderer was down. Joel winced, but he couldn't help thinking of the dead hunter. "Lefty, you may've just got your revenge," he said.

Then Soft Spot was heading back in Joel's direction. And the pony was loose and following her, transfigured—prancing, his neck arched, his eye bright and careless. They disappeared over the next hilltop, running as a team.

At this point, Joel didn't care much about the murderer. It had come to him that his stakes-winning half-sister to a Broodmare of the Year, in heat and with a large very soft follicle, was running loose with what they delicately call, out here, a

93

male horse. He'd been carefully calling the pony "it," to stave off his sense of impending doom. But he'd seen right away that it was an entire male horse. True, it was a short male horse, but Soft Spot was a short thoroughbred mare, and there were plenty of convenient hillsides nearby which would make a thoroughbred-pony liaison possible.

Joel could see his application for registration of foal next year—"Black, brown, chestnut, and white colt, out of Soft Spot, by Murderer's Pony."

Then he heard a voice—a deep, blues-shouting equine voice—a voice of authority. He heard Soft Spot's sweet, high reply, and a rapid-fire series of squeals, grunts, thuds, and finally the crunch of wood breaking. He put his hand to his head.

And the spotted pony reappeared, running toward Joel, transformed again. Chalk-eyed, his neck and shoulders lathered, he was suddenly the Pony Express coming down the road, and this pony was really hauling the mail.

Still, he was no match for his pursuer, though she was twenty-three years old. With her long, low, racey style, Miss Brown was literally eating him up, savaging him at every stride. All her old fury at these Pretenders, the spotted ponies of the world, had obviously boiled over onto this one hapless pony that had tried consorting with her daughter.

Then the murderer, who had unfortunately not been killed after all, came running back down the opposite hill, followed by his sons and the backing-up Buick. The pony looked up. Finding himself between the murderer and Miss Brown, he chose the murderer. At least, he went that way. Miss Brown went after him.

And so at last the murderer and his sons made the acquaintance of a truly wild horse. Eyes bulging, mule ears pinned, wicked head snaked out, teeth bared and snapping, Miss Brown slung herself straight at them.

They all propped, looking like they'd swallowed their

tongues. Then they ran behind the Buick. So did the pony. Miss Brown started chasing them around the car. The men would all dive for one door, screaming and shoving. The pony would pop up and try to get in the door, too, because Miss Brown was always right on top of him. The first man in would slam the door, and the others would have to run around the car again. The car was shuddering in place, belching smoke, and taking explosive hits from Miss Brown's hooves.

She loaded all three of the sons in the Buick that way, but then they either couldn't or wouldn't open a door for the murderer. Finally he staggered to the trunk of the car, yanked it open, and sat down in it. The engine backfired, the pony outbroke the Buick, and the murderer rode off backward in a puff of black smoke, chasing his pony again.

Soft Spot had come jogging up, looking amazed. She started to follow the pony, but Miss Brown headed her off, kicking her once, emphatically, and herded her back downhill toward Joel and the trailer.

So things were simpler now. No murderer, no pony, just one mare he couldn't catch, and one he couldn't load, both with no halters. And his spare halter, of course, was running off up the road with the pony.

Then Miss Brown charged at Joel. She knocked him aside, galloped straight into the trailer, turned her head around and gave him one of her "Hello?" looks, as if she'd been waiting all year to get in this trailer. She spoke to Soft Spot. Soft Spot stepped in beside her. Joel grabbed a stray piece of the murderer's rope, tied the tailgate in place, and the three of them went off to the breeding shed.

A year later, Joel's wife came dragging in from the barn at dawn. Soft Spot was overdue, and they'd been watching her day and night for a month. "She's running milk," his wife said. "Not dripping it, running it. Her butt looks pointy. She started pacing at one o'clock. By three, she looked real uncomfortable—digging up the stall, stomping her foot. She actually lay down, once, and I thought she was going to do it. At five, she quit pacing and started eating hay. I put her back in the paddock. But you know what? I think she's waiting to get out in the field with the other mares. I don't think she'll do it without Miss Brown."

"Of course," he groaned, as he struggled out of bed. "It's all a conspiracy, anyway."

Soft Spot was in the paddock behind the barn, where they could get to her quickly if she needed help foaling. She looked like a child's drawing of a horse—a round circle of a belly on four little stick legs. Joel checked her milk bag and her ligaments behind. "Trust me," he muttered in her ear. "You're ready for this." She gave him a perplexed, appealing glance, still the perfect horse ingenue—twelve months pregnant, and no idea what to do about it.

Beyond the fence, in the mare's field, stood Miss Brown, looking like a short fat vicious mule. After she'd saved her wayward daughter from the pony, Joel had brought her home to stay. For weeks she'd been hanging on the fence, waiting for Soft Spot to foal, as he was. What now? Should he call the veterinarian and get him to induce labor?

Joel walked up and looked into Miss Brown's ancient eyes. As he stared into that sphinxlike, brooding gaze, he suddenly saw Soft Spot, when she *was* just a tiny brown spot curled up in the middle of a big green field, her short little squirrel-tail switching up occasionally out of the grass, while the dark still block of Miss Brown watched over her. And it came to him that Miss Brown knew more than he did about Soft Spot's interminably interesting condition. She also knew more than he did about giving birth.

He went to the gate and opened it. "It'll probably take me two days to catch her," he said to himself. But Miss Brown came right to him, practically put her chin in his hand. He led her into the paddock. She and Soft Spot touched noses, greeting each other. Soft Spot dropped her head and started grazing. Miss Brown kept herself between Soft Spot and the other mares, who crowded the fence, watching.

Twenty minutes later, Soft Spot kicked at her belly twice and went down, breaking water. She lay, huge and sweating, helpless on the dewy grass. Miss Brown moved protectively behind her daughter. But when Joel squatted down between them, she did not offer to kick his head off. She only watched closely as he slid his hand inside the protruding white bubble of the birth sack, to make sure the foal was coming right. "Two front feet and a nose, and we're smelling like a rose," he told her. Then he stepped back.

Soft Spot began grunting the foal out, inch by inch—the soft, still jellylike feet, the blind muzzle, the floppy ears, the deep chest. And every time her daughter groaned and pushed, Miss Brown raised one foreleg, high and slow, and dug at the ground, as if she also felt the birth pang. One big push, one big dig—deliberately, painfully, patiently—till a tiny, chocolate-colored, mule-eared filly sat on the grass, checking out the world. Soft Spot reached her head around and sniffed the foal, her nostrils fluttering tenderly. "Huh-huh-huh-huh-huh!" she said, like she'd just figured it all out.

"Huh!" Joel agreed, like he'd figured out some of it, anyway. Because here they were—Soft Spot, with her first foal safely on the ground, and himself and Miss Brown, side by side, watching over them. Miss Brown stood head down, her knobby spine sticking up, showing her age, her whole body looking peaceful and spent, as if she herself had just dug this little creature out of the green earth.

97

# MAGIC LANTERN

The girl in a long dress—heavy fabric, military-looking, with braid—standing in front of a well with a bucket hung up behind her. The girl in a grape arbor, her wide, pale face among the leaves, the tendrils of her hair around her, like a nymph coming out of a grapevine. The girl stooping by water, a clear lake, her face among the pebbles, a lovely woman made out of stones. She squatted, picked up the pebbles, turned them over, a dark mass in her braided gown. Childlike in her perfect modular form, womanly, eternal, the legless tripod-goddess of the caves, carved out of stone forever, but with a human smile on her smooth, serious face.

No photographs of her nude. She seemed indeed very clothed, always, as the Flemish painters clothed their women with such knowledge of their draperies, part of their being secret, their actuality and sensuality. Her exposed skin was itself fine as silk, the lines of her body strong enough to make their revelations through a quilt.

99

Here was a photograph of just her nose and eyes and brow, cut off by the circle of a drum-cistern—a face as still and mysterious as the moon, as if she had no other life but this much of a face, and needed only that. All eyes, the bridge of her broad eccentric nose, the gleam of skin above the dark water as perfect as the face shining in the water below. You had to imagine the mouth. The face demanded you imagine it.

And here the back view, the girl disappearing on sand beside trees, as solid and lost a figure as you could ever bear to see. No further recession seemed possible. The slender upright trees, the bright bare light, her head a little forward, as if looking before her at where she must go, alone. The firm roundness of the shoulders under the braided jacket, the slight tip of the skirt to one side, all expressed resolve, motion against all desire. A needing to turn back. A knowing not to.

The girl emerging out of darkness, now. Her white smile, as she handed Charlotte a cup of tea.

They'd been smiling at each other in the halls, ever since the girl had moved into the apartment below Charlotte's. Today Charlotte had come down to borrow the girl's phone. And she was surprised to find that this girl, who had always seemed to be disappearing deliberately into the background, had an apartment full of photographs of herself, tacked up on the walls, laid out or stacked on the tables. Charlotte didn't believe in photography as art—she had a photographer friend with whom she'd debated this point for years. But when the girl had gone to get her the cup of tea, having kindly offered it, Charlotte had looked around her, and understood that if it were not art she was looking at, it was at least something magical going on.

For one thing, Charlotte thought, you couldn't see how extraordinary the girl was just by looking at her. Her smile was a giveaway, but her sturdy, almost-too-heavy body wasn't clear in its masses to the eye. But to the camera! To the camera you could see she had given not only body but soul. It was an act of generosity—no, of sacrifice—for to encounter her at all was to understand how private she was.

But in the way of a lot of private people, she had no defenses beyond the first clear line—had learned none of the twists and turns of those who don't mind giving themselves away a little, who even do it on purpose, to entertain themselves. So, when Charlotte asked her who had taken all the wonderful pictures, she stared around her slowly, as if noticing them for the first time. "John..." she said softly, as if to herself. "...Troy," she added gently, glancing at Charlotte.

Charlotte nodded, more interested in the way she'd said the name than in the name itself. "They're very compelling," she told the girl, in some surprise. The girl blinked at her, looking surprised herself. And then she told Charlotte the whole story.

"No one else has been here," she said at the end of it, smiling brightly, raising her hand in apology for the display. "I never thought..." As if there were nobody but herself left in the world!

That brightness, the finality of her smile—were they there all along? Or had she learned them, looking back through the lens to the man's eye that had dwindled, telescoped into just that— an eye, like the eye of God? Did she still move in it, even now that her famous photographer-lover was dead? Was that what gave such weight to her motion, such graveness to her smile? In the pictures it was as if she wanted to remember him, as if he were the subject and she the portraitist, so straight and whole was her gaze. As if she could preserve him from the dissolve that had waited for him, by the light of her glance flashing on him or holding steady. Or as if by standing before his flickering lens, she had dissolved herself into that other world he was going to, become herself the photograph, given it such soul that it had, as they say, stepped off the page. And into the beyond.

The photographs with their look of long-ago, that brownish nostalgic tinge, as if they'd been put away in a drawer lovingly and forever. The wallpapered walls of the apartment, with tiny lights in sconces like a Spanish castle, and the sense that you could have developed *anything* in there. Fish might have swum in the air, it was so thick from the shades and the vines that covered the windows, and the girl came and went, sinking into the shadows, drifting up again, eyes first. That weighted tip of her body as she took Charlotte's cup and turned away, as if she were caught forever in her dead lover's last photograph. The magazines and books under the lamp, all his—what he'd read, what he'd written.

"When you start respecting the dead," Charlotte told the girl as she left, "then they're really dead. You've got to keep arguing with them."

"I never did argue with him," the girl murmured apologetically.

"No?" Charlotte said, looking at the white, serious smile, then around her at all the pictures of that smile. "Well, maybe you ought to start."

Afterward, Charlotte realized it was not just because she'd asked about the photographs that the girl had confided in her. It was also because, when the girl told her the man's name, Charlotte hadn't reacted at all, obviously hadn't recognized it.

But once she left, it came to her. She'd seen that name on books in her old friend Hugh's house, heard it invoked in their long-term debate about the value of photography. She remembered that he'd published a monograph on John Troy, and he'd been sad for a whole day after he'd heard the man had died. Charlotte was sad for a whole day herself, thinking of the girl alone in that dim apartment, drifting among his relics. The next morning, she called Hugh and asked him to lunch, saying she had a new student for his photography class.

The girl had never actually said, "Don't tell anybody." *Still*—this was such a delicate matter—the girl's privacy at stake. Charlotte shook her head sternly, both at herself and at Hugh. She'd resolved *not* to give him the famous man's name.

But Hugh shook his head back at her. "She doesn't *need* my class, then, if she's studied with 'someone *distinguished*,'" he said, half-piqued, half-mocking her. "This class is for beginners."

"She *is* a beginner," Charlotte said. "She needs to become . . . something. And this is all she knows to become. I don't think it matters right now what kind of photography she does."

Hugh stared at her in disbelief, which was, it occurred to her, what their friendship was founded on. As good a basis as any, she told herself. They could never misunderstand each other, since they knew from the outset that they had no assumptions in common. As usual, she'd have to explain everything.

It was a good thing she was so good at explaining. By the time she was through telling him what she'd seen in the girl's apartment, she didn't have to give him the photographer's name.

"Troy—but it *can't* be!"

Hugh wouldn't believe it, at first, though he was the one who'd said the name. Charlotte answered his excited questions patiently, even when he asked them over and over; she was, she had to admit, enjoying what seemed to be the climactic astonishment of their friendship. No one had even seen this particular girl, Hugh said. They had seen other girls, of course— apparently many others; had viewed them, over the years, in the great man's shows, in his books.

Charlotte thought of generations of lovely young women, rolled into his magic box and come out flat, one-dimensional, with a finality they never had in the flesh. Developed forever in that state of youth, all time forward an illusion of that time. Displayed forever so.

But no one had even *heard* of these last photographs, Hugh said. Did the famous photographer wait, Charlotte wondered, not have that last show because he lost interest, couldn't care about it any more? Or did he decide, more likely—since he kept on taking the pictures—that it ought to be complete, a full chronicle of the girl's movement from innocence and joy to loss, love as terrible and completed knowledge? A dramatic perspective, all right.

"It's a young girl looking at the end of the world," she said, summing up. "Straight at it. An innocent girl."

"How come *you're* so moved?" Hugh said. He'd calmed down enough to lean back and grin at her sardonically. "It's just doing the wrong thing at the right moment, isn't it?" All great photographs, she had told him once, were that.

"*He* may've been. But she wasn't. What she was doing was right. That makes the difference. I don't care if he was real or not. *She* was."

"She *was?* She's not any more?"

"Not like that. I don't think you can do that more than once in your life. And of course now she's not innocent any more. Never to be private again...," she said like a lament.

Hugh had taken off his glasses and was rubbing his nose, briskly, where they pinched. "Who has the negatives?" he asked, blinking, looking sleepy.

"Why, she does. I'm sure."

"So—" he stared down into his glasses, rubbing them—"why are you worried about her privacy? She could just..."

Charlotte shook her head. "She'll never be able to destroy them. She'll have to show them eventually, publish them. Even if it weren't who it is—she knows what she's got. You could tell that just by the way they were arranged on the tables. She has eyes. An eye." *His* eye?

The fishlike eye swimming upward from the depths to blink slowly, and re-descend.

"It hardly seems possible to me," Charlotte went on, "that he could've kept it up."

"Kept what up?"

"Kept taking the damn things. He *knew* he was dying, after all," she said irritably.

"He should've gone straight, there at the end?"

"You'd think he'd come to a moment when he'd just want to look at her. Himself."

"That's how he did it."

She shook her head. She would never believe that. "That poor girl," she said. "It seems like an enormity to me. He never could've looked at her once, or he would've seen . . ." The white, final smile, the back trudging away, obedient, touching. How could he not have dropped the camera, run to her—called her to him, if he couldn't run?—if he couldn't call, at least set the camera down? Never take the picture? "If it hadn't been for that box with the evil eye in it . . ." Charlotte shook her head again. She had a very primitive notion of cameras.

"But the photographs, you say, are . . ."

Charlotte stared at him. Sighed. Nodded. "Supernatural. That's what. Pictures taken by a ghost. Or of a ghost. What her ghost will be. What she is now—a kind of ghost."

The girl was showing Charlotte the great man's collection of antique cameras. One of them was like Charlotte's grandfather's camera; she remembered the wink of light inside the dark, startling, internal-feeling. "It's like sex," she said to Barbara. That was the girl's name. "Like after sex. You know." She couldn't bring herself to explain.

"Oh—yes," Barbara said, with the white smile. "Yes. I see what you mean."

"I wonder if men ever think of that," Charlotte said.

"Of sex? About cameras? Yes. I know they do. But not that way, I think. You'd have to be a woman..."

"Magic lanterns, they used to call those old slide projectors," Charlotte mused. "People like for things to be magic, you know. Rather than real. If you can *call* it that," she added, sniffing a little, looking around her at all the photographs.

Barbara looked around her, too. "I can't call it anything any more," she said. "It's just...what's here."

"*You're* what's here," Charlotte said, smiling.

"Am I?" Barbara asked, a curious note in her voice. She raised both arms a little, ducking her head as if to look at herself and see. But her eyes went shut, like a doll's. Charlotte first thought the girl was going to cry. Then she thought she herself was going to cry. The heaviness in the symmetrically lifted arms, the stillness of the sturdy female body, the white part dividing surgically the dark heavy hair—God save us, Charlotte said to herself—it's another photograph. Maybe he couldn't help himself.

Certainly the girl couldn't help herself. Charlotte, on the other hand—"Let's walk over to school," she said, finding her coat, putting it on. "I want you to do something for me. Well, really for a friend of mine."

She told Barbara that Hugh was having trouble filling his class. The truth was, he was trying to keep people out of it. "Don't listen to a word he says," Charlotte said. "I never do. Just sign up for the class, and go, at least in the beginning. I know this man," she said firmly. "I'll tell him to leave you alone."

"I'm going to treat her just like anybody else in the class," Hugh said threateningly. "No matter how much she knows. She'll be starting all over again, at the beginning."

"Why are you resisting this so, Hugh? Are you afraid she'll know more than you do? Because I can tell you right now, she does."

"I just don't see what good it'll do either of us for her to be in my class," he said sulkily.

"All right," she said. "I'll tell you what good. She was doing all the developing alone, I gather, that last year. Think of it. Seeing your own face, your own bones, glowing in the dark—"

"What was he shooting?" Hugh said. "X-rays?"

"And *now*—" Charlotte went on, "she's afraid to be alone in the darkroom. She told me so, the first time I talked to her."

He stared at her, eyes wide. Then laughed, one short sharp laugh. Pure disbelief. But she had gotten his attention. "And as for *you*," she went on, smiling at him sweetly, "don't tell me you don't want to see all those pretty pictures on her walls."

Hugh shrugged, looking at her sidelong as they got up to leave. "I figured I'd stop by your place sometime, let you introduce me." She shook her head. "There's a Photography Club," he went on. "I'll take her. Introduce her. I'll even stay for the meeting."

Charlotte went on shaking her head. "This girl isn't ready to join the human race. Much less the Photography Club. No, the class is just right. I told her you won't even know she's there."

"I won't even know she's there," Hugh repeated in an awed tone, nodding a little, his head on one side. Then looked away and laughed, a stagy, incredulous laugh.

Charlotte sized him up as she walked out with him. One of the things she could never believe about Hugh was that he was tall. Sitting down, he sank in his chair and was short, a little man with a lot of wild grey-black hair like charcoal scribbling around his face, a big nose, and a moustache. She quite liked him short. She could look right across at him and see him, behind his glasses, blinking at her with his dark, sad-dog-bad-dog eyes. But on his feet, with his glasses off, he was impressive, a tall man with a noble profile, black moustaches drooping down at her splendidly. In the flamboyant clothes he affected—which suited him, she had to admit—he had a kind of costume-drama glamour. With a little more shoulder, and a little less of a slouch, he would have made a dashing cavalier, she said to herself. Or a handsome footman. She sighed. "I do what I have to do," she said, half to herself.

Charlotte asked Barbara up one evening, so they could talk. Away from the shrine, she said to herself. Offered a drink, Barbara asked for tea. "Don't drink?" Charlotte said.

Barbara shook her head. "I used to smoke a lot," she said. "Before I met John. He wanted everything—straight. No drink, no dope—"

No back-talk from his protégées, Charlotte said to herself. To Barbara she said, "Doesn't sound like the photographers *I* know."

Barbara smiled, in her gentle, apologetic way, "He had to take so much stuff, the last year. So many pills. So many shots. 'Clarity is all we've got,' he used to say." Charlotte nodded, understanding, in spite of herself. "He didn't believe in distortion for effect," Barbara added, her voice rising and trembling—fervent, almost defensive.

"Well well," Charlotte said soothingly. "Who does?"

"Oh a lot of people," Barbara said seriously. "A lot of them are more interested in what they can make of the image than in the image itself."

"You mean..." Charlotte said, "like looking at the Christmas tree?" Barbara smiled at her blankly. "That's what my sister and I used to call it," Charlotte explained. "We'd make our eyes go blurry, so we couldn't see all those ugly little wires and light bulbs on the tree. If you look too hard at things, of course, you're always being disappointed by the world."

"He *wasn't*, though," Barbara said, drawing herself up, the

108

pride of her old love come back on her whole for a moment. "That was the whole thing. He *loved* the world. He loved *seeing* it."

"Must have loved seeing you, anyway," Charlotte said, smiling at her. Seeing, faraway, the clarity of that gaze he had moved in, his last year—as simple, as pure, as straight as daylight. How she must have saved him, from all the darkness and distortion of disease and treatment. Willing to look back at him forever, in his little black box, his secret last waiting place. Willing to give up her soul for his. No wonder, Charlotte said to herself, she has trouble raising her arms, these days,

Still, on the face of it, Charlotte could hardly urge bourbon and water. "How's Hugh?" she asked instead. "How's your class?"

But it seemed, from the silent blush that was Barbara's only response, that they'd just been discussing that question. Remembering some odd, blurred pictures she'd seen tacked up on Hugh's wall—"I *told* you not to listen to anything he said," Charlotte said, shaking her head at the girl.

Barbara smiled her white smile, looking relieved, even animated. "But he's *your* friend," she said, shaking her head back. "And I do like him. You mustn't think I don't."

"Liking them is one thing," Charlotte said. "Listening to them is another. And as for Hugh being my friend—" but now Barbara was listening to *her*, head cocked; and how could she explain to a girl just past twenty-one the ironies of middle-age, when you find that keeping your friends sometimes requires giving up on them? Charlotte raised her eyes to the ceiling. "That was before I knew he was capable of distortion for effect."

Charlotte came into Hugh's apartment for the first time in a long time. A party was going on there, and he'd invited his class. He opened the door and then swung back to continue photographing a couple who were dancing. "I see you've got your crocodile mask on," Charlotte said, eying with distaste the arrangement of metal and plastic that looked to be screwed to his forehead. "Don't you point that thing at me," she told him, as he turned the camera on her menacingly.

They stood together and watched Barbara as she talked to some of Hugh's other students. She was wearing a black tee shirt with her jeans tonight—half-mourning, Charlotte said to herself; it became her. "A lovely girl," Charlotte said, proud of Barbara for talking, proud of herself and Hugh for getting her some people to talk to.

"A lovely young woman," he said sanctimoniously, correcting her.

She slid her eyes over at him. "A girl is a perfectly all-right thing to be, when you're the right age for it. I was one myself once. And I knew you when you called us all chicks. Or ladies."

"You'll always be a lady to me, Charlotte," he said, smiling at her maliciously.

"You'd better hope so," she said. "I might start telling the little chic-kies all your secrets."

"I don't have any secrets," he said, raising his camera and pointing it at Barbara, glancing at Charlotte once over it. Bad-dog tonight, she said to herself.

"That's the first thing I'll tell them," she told him, as he clicked the shutter.

Later in the evening, she saw Hugh and Barbara standing together at a round table with a big book open on it. Charlotte knew the book; it was one of the places she'd remembered seeing John Troy's name. Hugh leaned over it, his two hands flat on the table, his weight forward, his shoulders squared by that forthright posture, his head turned up to look at Barbara as he spoke. Her straight gaze was on him, not the book. But the fingers of both her hands touched the edge of the table delicately, as if a spirit might speak to her out of it, or as if she could feel the photographs, feel them with her fingertips in the wood of the table. Or as if, by that light touch, she were trying to keep her balance.

Watching this tableau, Charlotte made up her mind to go home early.

But she was glad to hear, in the days following, a lighter sound to Barbara's footsteps, a little brightness in her voice. She asked Charlotte a few questions, shyly, about Hugh. How long had she known him? Had he ever been married? "Forever," Charlotte said; and "Oh millions of times." Barbara nodded wisely, as if she'd figured as much. She knew about his past shows, Charlotte noted, talked about the next one knowledgeably. The class, she said, was helping him print some of the photographs for it. At one point, she admitted that Hugh was giving her special attention. "Oh dear," Charlotte said, raising her eyebrows.

"Of course," Barbara said, "he had to see that I—know a little. But it's embarrassing, sometimes. I feel like I'm...on false pretenses."

"Ah well," Charlotte said, wagging her head. "Aren't we all?"

But then she had to ponder, under Barbara's grave eyes, what possibilities remained for truth-telling at this point. She looked away, to the other faces of this girl, her other life. Shadows on paper, now, it still had an undeniable truth to it, so much that in this room the girl herself would always recede somewhat before it. In the face of indefinite recession, Charlotte found herself not anxious to opt for truth. Truth was one thing, life another. And Hugh had one great virtue—he was alive. "Blame me," she said at last, shrugging, meeting that straight look head-on. "I'm the one running the ringer here. If anyone is."

Then Barbara announced that Hugh was taking her to the Photography Club meeting that Friday night. Charlotte nodded, a little wearily. So he would get to see the pictures, in his uningenious way, after all. Barbara looked at her, inquiring.

"You know he's way too young for you," Charlotte said, cocking an eye at her.

"Well of course," Barbara said, giggling, blushing, looking half-delighted, half-shocked at herself, "compared to John—"

"I meant compared to you," Charlotte said, holding her eyes.

Barbara's gaze turned grave again. "That scares me," she said. And Charlotte said nothing more.

But she came right down, Saturday morning, for a visit. The shades were up, the apartment seemed strangely bright. Charlotte stood blinking in the door at three brand-new photographs, still-lifes of someone's kitchen. All the other walls, all the tables were clear and bare. My God, she said to herself— a clean sweep. Did he carry them all off with him the first night? To Barbara she said, "What did they *do* to you at the Photography Club, anyway?"

"Oh. I did this before," Barbara said coolly, looking around her. In the light she had a new solidity, a new alertness in her stance. "Yesterday afternoon. Hugh was coming to pick me up, you know."

She was right, of course, Charlotte thought—and more tactful than Charlotte had expected her to be. What a shock it would be to a man who was interested in a woman to walk, like that, into her former life. And such a life—"tragic"—"distinguished"—as he'd never dreamt of for her. If he hadn't known it all along, that is. As it was, it must have been another sort of shock. Poor Hugh, Charlotte thought—so desperate to see the great man's pictures, then faced with all these blank surfaces, relieved only by fish and cauliflower. Charlotte herself was not quite able to take it in, kept turning from one stripped wall to another.

"It's *strange* in here," she said. "I mean, it was strange before, but now—" she turned to Barbara suddenly. "You didn't burn them or something, did you?" she whispered. She was more bothered than she would have expected to be by the thought.

112

"Oh no," the girl said calmly. "I just filed them away. For now." But Charlotte was shocked, then, at the businesslike tone of her voice, the detachment of her gaze. Photography captures the soul, savages believe; Charlotte believed it, too, obviously, at least enough to protest it. If you're a photographer, Hugh would say, that's your business.

And if you haven't got a soul of your own, Charlotte said to herself—

But this girl did. And she'd filed it away. For now.

After that, Charlotte did not see much of either Hugh or Barbara. Barbara's disappearance, like that of the pictures, was both a loss and a relief to Charlotte. She found herself suddenly in too many different positions in this affair. It was not an unfamiliar feeling. She was in the habit of knowing too much about her friends' lives.

But one night, coming in from out of town and seeing the lights on in Barbara's apartment, she knocked on the door, by impulse, and thought she heard a faint voice telling her to come in. The sweet smell she still associated with the little dried-grass baskets she'd woven in her childhood hung inside the door like an airlock. Hugh was sitting on the floor, Barbara on the couch behind him, drooping over him, his head back on her knees. Charlotte sat on the end of the couch, and she and Hugh chatted a little, Hugh quieter and pleasanter than usual. There were a lot of silences. Barbara, meanwhile, scrabbled around with her fingers in the wild nest of Hugh's hair, staring down into it as if fascinated. When Charlotte found herself noticing the way each of Hugh's dark hairs was sunburnt red at the end—a detail which had escaped her in all their years of friendship—she got herself up and out of there. Barbara had never looked up or spoken.

———

Barbara and Hugh married the next summer, up East, at his parents' home. Their book on John Troy's last photographs appeared that winter, along with a big show in New York. Charlotte saw them occasionally at local parties, and got her usual invitation when Hugh had his next show.

His photographs of Barbara—and there were a great many of them, of course, in the show—were of a perfectly ordinary young woman, attractive, slightly overweight. A little strain showing in her face, sometimes, Charlotte thought—a kind of spasm, looking like an accident, the wrong light, a momentary tic. But it might have been, for all Charlotte knew, a trick of the photograph itself—distortion for effect.

She saw, for a moment, the ghost of the famous photographer rising up wrathful out of the developing tray, saying not like that, you fool. Too much light, too little. Your focus is all wrong. You're killing her.

Still, there was Barbara, not killed at all. Blooming, in fact. Pregnant, in fact. Hugh would at last have the family to match his moustache. She smiled her white smile at Charlotte, quite kindly, from across the room.

He would never have noticed her on his own, Charlotte said to herself. You could tell that from the photographs. But he would want her always, now, for the same reason the first man had wanted her—to look back at him forever, beyond fame and photography, with her grave dark eyes.

And here was Hugh, tall and newly distinguished in a somber black suit, coming over to embrace Charlotte, as much as he ever did, one squeeze of her shoulder, too hard. "You've *got* to come by and see us," he said. "After all, you're the one who..." he grinned down at her cozily. "Barbara's even forgiven you, by now, for telling me about John."

Charlotte's head jerked back. She stared up at her old friend

Hugh, who blinked down at her once, sleepily, his eyes like glass. "*Forgiven* me!" she said, laughing, in final disbelief.

But then she turned away, her stomach sinking, believing it all. The question was, she knew, whether she would ever forgive herself.

# GRASS FIRES

I t was small, like cats and dogs are small, down at Jimmie's knees. It moved in a ragged line, and in back of it was black, and in front of it was grey dry grass. It moved without much noise or smoke, its little red flames walking up the ridge no faster than he could walk, but no slower either. And it was long, like a long red snake stretching itself sideways. It moved on its own, it went where it liked. Wherever the dry grass was it went, and there was a world of dry grass, now. It didn't hurt the grass to burn. The grass couldn't feel it.

Then the big red fire engine came bellowing up the road, jumping the potholes, its ladders and hoses leaning, and the hoses pulled free and the beautiful red truck roared right into the field, and everybody who came by stopped their cars and trucks and got out to pound on the fire with jackets or shovels or whatever they could find, trying to stay ahead of the line of red, that kept growing another loop, so they had to run over and push it back again. The fire engine went in front of them, shooting rainbows of spray into the air, hissing the fire out. And Jimmie was up there fighting it with them, scratching it out with his rake, fast as he could go.

Everybody stood around afterwards and talked.

"Lots of these fires now, on the TV," Mr. Johnson, from down the road, said. "In Canada."

Mr. Baxter, from across the fence, said, "The Australians have some serious grass fires going."

Mr. Johnson nodded. "That's right, the Australians. In Canada."

The Fire Chief said they were not supposed to be burning. "We got the alert on, you know, Mr. Crawley," he told Jimmie's daddy, pointing to their smoky trash burner. "We might ought to cite you."

"I burn every Saturday," Jimmie's daddy said. "Wasn't that much trash, anyway."

The Fire Chief shook his head. "Just a spark is all it takes, in this kind of weather. The whole world is ready to burn."

The next day there was another fire, on Mr. Crump's place, across the road. Mr. Crump was Jimmie's daddy's enemy. The little piece of ground where the fire started was what they were enemies over. The fire jumped up in the trees this time and burned a ways into Johnson's woods. Laney Johnson was scared it might follow the woods down the ridge to her Uncle Luke's house, and him blind, and couldn't see it. But the fire engine came back again, and they stopped it at the pond.

After that, there was a fire almost every day. Just little ones. Early in the mornings, when nobody was looking, the shadows slipped out of the cedars, down where the ridges cracked together. He knew who they were, moving like his own shadow—stooping, setting little heaps of grass on fire, one here, one there. The burning grass crumbled and twisted and glared.

And the fires were moving away now, further away—down

the road, through the fence lines. The wind was blowing, the whole world was ready to burn, the Australians had some serious grass fires going, in Canada, all over. A bunch of people had got killed, on the TV.

But these little fires hadn't hurt anybody except trees. The beautiful red fire engine always came out in the fields and sprayed its rainbows, everybody came, and they all fought the fires together. Saving the long-necked horses on Mr. Baxter's farm, that used to be their blackberry patch, till he bought it and bush-hogged all the brambles. Saving the hay rolls for the Sims' cattle. Lonnie Sims and him had had the accident, their trucks banged together in the road like two bulls butting heads. Saving Mrs. Thayer's house. It was her grandson Bart had let his rabbits aloose, so maybe she didn't deserve to be saved. But they saved her anyway.

Then one day, even the fire engine couldn't get to the fire. It was in the woods, and the cedar trees kept going up with big whooshes, it was jumping from tree to tree. Too much fire for the truck, they said. He didn't understand why the truck couldn't go up there, but they said it couldn't. The fire had got away from them.

---

The day after the fire got loose in the woods, burning a black swath of trees and grass all the way down to the next road, Sydney Crump phoned Frank Baxter. "We need to get the law in on this," he said, in his high jumpy voice. Sydney had been in the service, and he had a great respect for the law. "I called the Sheriff. Told him who's doing it."

"We don't *know* who's doing it," Frank said.

"We sure as hell do," Sydney said. "Everybody knows."

They were all used to seeing Jimmie Crawley marching up

and down Sorter Ridge Road—a big stout man carrying a tobacco stick, digging it into the dirt at the edge of the road. He'd grin and wave that stick at everybody who drove by.

And everybody did drive by. They knew if they felt sorry for him and stopped to speak, he'd just say something like, "Seen any flying cars lately?" Then he'd laugh and laugh, a high wild laugh that went on way too long for anybody to be comfortable with.

But when there was a fire, they all stopped. And Jimmie was always there, with his red excited face and gleaming eyes—first to every fire, and fighting it like a demon. All the people who'd had a fire could remember some recent history they'd had with him or his family. And old Edna Fite, who had the longest memory of anybody, hinted at a history of fires past. "Always knew *he'd* start *that* again," she growled.

So the Sheriff came out and talked to everybody, and then he told them there was nothing he could do. "We got no evidence, no witnesses," he said, apologetically. "Just circumstantial and hearsay."

Sydney Crump lost some of his respect for the law: "Well, that boy better be real careful," he said. "I got a whole lot of brothers here, and some of them are hostile."

That was no lie. One of Sydney's brothers had shot and killed a strip-mine bulldozer operator up in the mountains, protecting the Crump family graveyard. And that brother was free and living with Sydney, his crime having been judged murder in a good cause.

The fires were out of control, and it felt like everything and everybody else was about to be. Smoke hung over Sorter Ridge like a stain in the sky, the air smelled scorched, even at night, and the figure of Jimmie Crawley, grinning and waving his tobacco stick, moved in the background of all their nightmares.

"Why doesn't someone talk to Mase and Aline?" Frank Baxter's wife asked him. "They're his parents."

But of course everybody was trying real hard *not* to talk to Jimmie's parents. It was one of those things people don't want to mention—"We think you're son's the firebug."

"Why don't we call Virginia Dougherty?" Frank's wife went on. "They're old friends of the Crawleys. And she's a neutral party—they don't live out here any more."

But Virginia Dougherty maintained, in her fresh, gentle, well-spoken way, that they all were wrong about Jimmie. "People misunderstand him, because he's—the way he is. But you know, his mother calls me every day about those fires—she's scared to death of them," Virginia told Frank. "I just can't believe he's the one doing it."

"I don't *want* to believe it," Frank said, "but everybody else sure does. The truth is, if he could prove he was at a basketball game in town every time a fire started, they'd all still think it's him, just because he is a little retarded."

There was a silence, like he'd said something he shouldn't have. Then Virginia said she'd see what she could do.

———

"But there's been nothing like that, not for years and years," Virginia said to herself, as she drove up to Sorter Ridge. "And he was so much younger then."

There at the top of the hill were the steps to the old school. It had been "the old school" even when Virginia was growing up—unused for years, just part of the landscape, but still square and upright. Then one afternoon it had burnt flat to the ground, only the steps left standing. Walking up now to an empty field, to empty sky.

An old outbuilding burned down, shortly after that, on Edna Fite's place. Edna's grandkids had told her Jimmie was playing with matches. Edna had yelled at him so loud, Virginia could make out every word from half a mile away. Aline had come running down to Virginia's house, in tears: "He's just a poor little innocent child."

"When *I* was about his age," Virginia had told her, "Sue Ellen Cartwright and I hid out in the stripping room every day after school—taking turns, lighting one, letting it burn down almost to our fingers, then lighting another, till we went through a whole box of kitchen matches. It's a wonder we didn't burn the barn down." She'd suggested that Aline keep Jimmie home, till the talk died out. It did, and there'd been no more fires.

Till now. Here were the steep, shining pastures of Sorter Ridge, their thick silver thatch upturned to the winter sun, and all of them slashed by the dark jagged scars of grass fires.

"He gets the blame for everything," Aline had told her bitterly, back when those old buildings burned. That was when Aline gave up and took him out of school. If it was now, Virginia said to herself, there'd be some special class for a kid like Jimmie. But there was nothing like that, back then. He just kept failing.

Plus, Aline was afraid to let him go. She was always afraid. It was like having Jimmie had made her afraid. She never knew what was going to happen next. She expected things to go wrong. He'd failed so many grades, he was a whole lot bigger than the other kids in his class, still trying to play with them, getting into fights. "The kids pick on him, and the teachers do too. And I know what they say—they say it's all my fault," Aline had told Virginia, crying again.

They'd both cried when Virginia moved to town, but Virginia was crying mostly for Aline. Virginia's kids were in junior high then, always wanting her to drive them to town for games and dances, and it was just easier to live there. And now that her kids were grown up and out on their own, she and Sam had bought the little iris nursery, and she ran it. Her life had gone on, and Aline's had stopped, because of Jimmie.

They'd been together in the pride of their first pregnancies, shy and vain of their swelling new bodies, full of life. They'd consulted about heat rash and teething, watched each other's kids. Jimmie had been a beautiful toddler, those bright blue eyes and that fine fair hair, then a pink-faced little boy who called her Aunt Birdie, and loved her Rice Krispie cookies. He still did.

But her kids had grown up, and he hadn't. It was such a sorrow to Aline, she knew, but Aline never talked about it any more. Her eyes just always looked a little more holed-up, her lips pressed tighter together, from not saying.

And after all these years, Virginia had to bring up the subject—had to tell Aline what they were blaming her son for now! She prayed to Jesus to let her say the right thing.

Here was the Crawley's small frame house, their little yard clean and neat, the way Mase always kept it. His car was gone. He'd be at the Square D, where all the farmers worked overtime on the line, trying to make a living; they did their farming in the evenings, raising "moon tobacco."

"Thank God you come," Aline said, as they hugged, and Virginia felt a little sink of guilt, knowing Aline thought she'd come just to comfort her about the fires. There was something hopeless even in Aline's hug, sagging away, like she wasn't quite there. She looked beat-down, dark patches under her eyes, her round, pretty face gone crooked with worry. "I don't understand why they cain't catch him," she said sharply. Then she drifted back to her perfectly clean kitchen, turning from one window to another in a slow, dreamy dance, staring out at the fields. "It's like they start all by theirselves," she sang, in a high, little-girl voice. "One minute there ain't one, then there one is."

Virginia went and looked out with her. There was Mase's barn, his farm machinery, and his hay rolls, all lined up one behind the other out their ridge top, like a train on a track. The old heaped-up hills stretched beyond.

"Oh looky there." Virginia pointed at Mase's pickup, to distract Aline from the black burn marks snaking up the hills. "Mase still has his sign." For Mase's birthday one year, Virginia had painted him a special sign, because he and Jimmie always drove together in that beat-up truck, with a broom stuck up in the back of it, like in the old TV program about the junkman: "SANFORD AND SON," the sign read. Even Aline had to giggle about that sign. Mase had hung it proudly on his tailgate, and he and Jimmie rode around for years like that.

"Must be hard on Jimmie, now he can't drive any more," Virginia went on, trying to find some way toward her subject. "I bet he feels cooped up." Jimmie never did have a license, but he was always crazy about trucks, and he'd learned to drive early, the way country kids do—first on the farm, then on the narrow roads around home.

Aline gave a helpless shrug. "You know Mase always wanted him to be...and he went *with* him, every time, in the beginning. And then we figured, well, out *here*...but of course them Simses claimed the accident was all his fault—said he was driving in the middle of the road."

"Well? I bet they *both* were. These old roads only *have* middles," Virginia said, shrugging and laughing.

Aline didn't even smile. "The Sheriff said he'd have to put him in jail, if we ever let him drive again. He'd go out there and start the truck, sit in it for hours, the engine running. I had to scare him so bad—tell him the Sheriff would come take him away from us, lock him up in a cage..." She stared out the window, her voice dropped down. "I'd die if he had to go to jail."

Virginia took a deep breath. *Now*, she told herself. "What time of day do the fires usually start?" she asked Aline.

"Always of a morning. I wake up every day smelling smoke. But Jimmie's outside before light, and never seen a soul. I reckon they're sneaking in from the back country, through the

124

woods." She was shifting past the windows again, her eyes wide. "They know when to do it, too—when we ain't watching. They're waiting to get us. Laughing at us. I can feel them out there, right now. Awaiting."

"But it *will* rain, you know," Virginia said, falling back on the weather for hope or blame, out of old country habit. "It always does."

"That's what Mase keeps saying. 'Ain't nothing but little grass fires.' But if they reach that barn," Aline waved a finger at the old tobacco barn that stood twenty feet from the house, "dry as tinder, with the wind blowing through the siding—"

"We often have a spell like this, between the winter snows and the spring rains. Things *get* dry. You've just got to be careful."

"But—they're *setting* these fires," Aline said, squeezing her eyes shut, like she was trying to imagine it, or not imagine it.

Virginia sighed and nodded. "It's not just somebody flipping their cigarette out the car window. They're doing it on purpose." She couldn't save Aline, or herself, from that truth.

"Them Crump boys," Aline muttered, shaking her head. "Sydney's brothers. Wander all over this place, say they're looking for their hounds. Looking to burn us out, more like.

"But Jimmie watches over me," she went on, with a pinched smile. "Says he ain't gonna let them get me. My poor little boy. And me here alone with him, all day. We cain't get away from them." Aline had never learned to drive, had been afraid of that too, though Virginia had tried to teach her.

"It does you no good to think like that."

Aline drew near the window, her gaze fixed suddenly. The frightened eyes. "Here he comes. He's out there all the time, now. But he'll come in to see *you*."

Jimmie came over the hill with his fast heavy rolling walk, too much motion in it, like somebody walking hard with no place to go, nothing to do but walk. Walking to no purpose. Or was he? He stared around him, his head screwed this way and that, like he expected to see someone or something. Virginia found herself scanning the air above the hills, wondering if the fire would show itself again. "Do you remember," she murmured, seeing his quick approach, "back when the old school burned down?"

Aline nodded, her eyes tearing over. "Now that was the sign from God. I knew it then, I got to keep him home, take care of him myself—always, always," she crooned. "And now he's taking care of me," she added, her voice shooting way up high, both her hands waving at him as he came in.

He gave Virginia a loving hug, clinging to her an extra minute, still just like a kid. "Seen about them fires, Aunt Birdie?" he asked her, happily. "On the TV?"

"Them ones on the TV ain't *here*, honey," Aline corrected him.

He nodded way up and down, like he knew better. "Fire engine come up here."

"He loves that fire engine," Aline said, patting his shoulder. "Don't you, honey?"

"We got the alert on," he told Virginia, nodding importantly.

Aline dropped down in a chair. "They been all around us now, every place but ours. We're next, I know it."

He put his arm around her, grinned into her face. "We got the alert on."

She stared off, talking in that little-girl voice. "You never know which way the wind'll be blowing. They'll come up here and take the house and us in it, some morning, and we'll never even know they're coming. These things move so quiet. We'll wake up burning in our beds."

"We got the alert on." He took up Aline's dance, watching out the windows. He did look more alert than Virginia had ever seen him—stamping back and forth, frowning at the world, with his head jerked forward and his lips pushed out. His movements were too loud for the small room, his color too high for Aline's pale pink tea-roses wallpaper.

"What do you do, on alert?" Virginia asked him, offhand. "I hear you get out there before daylight."

Aline jumped up. "Look at your hair," she said to Jimmie. "Out there in that wind, with no hat on." She whipped a comb out of her shirt pocket and went to combing his hair, which was down in his eyes, and he did look rough. He stopped in his tracks, leaning down to her automatically when she reached up on tiptoes to make the part. He had to bend way over. She did it slowly and carefully, brushing his hair softly off his forehead with her hand. He shut his eyes, like he was almost lulled to sleep.

Virginia stared out the window at the fire-tracks on the hills, feeling like she wasn't here, or shouldn't be. *They know just how how to do this*, she said to herself, half-angry, half-sad. *Aline's been combing his hair like that for thirty-two years.*

But Jimmie sat down with them then, groomed and docile, and ate a dozen of Virginia's Rice Krispie cookies. He thanked her politely, the way he always did, and stood up again, big and proud. "We got the alert on."

Aline pointed a finger. "Where's your hat?" she asked him. He turned and wandered obediently toward his room. From the back, Virginia thought, he looked exactly like his father, like a middle-aged man—that slight stoop showing early in his round shoulders, the way it did in Mase's shoulders, once he began to see his strapping firstborn son was never growing up.

"How's Buddy?" Virginia asked Aline. Buddy was Jimmie's younger brother, who was smart and lively, and used to work with him on the farm. But as soon as Buddy finished school, he'd gone off into the Army. "I bet Jimmie misses him," Virginia added, looking once more for an opening.

"Buddy comes, and he goes," Aline said, faraway. She watched in silence as Jimmie disappeared into his room. Then she turned and looked Virginia in the eye. "*He'll* never leave us," she said hoarsely, with a fierce, proud, terrified glare.

Virginia felt that look. *She'd* left them, of course. As Buddy had done. As everyone else had done. And even Mase went off to his job, five days a week. They'd all left Aline alone with Jimmie, all these years. What right did Virginia have to question her about what he might have done? She couldn't believe it herself, anyway. And Aline must have made that choice, too, at some moment, whether she'd known it or not. He was her life, in a way.

He came back, making for the front door, with that jolting, hasty walk. Still no hat.

Aline started up. "You wait right there. It's cold out." She went straight off to get his hat. Jimmie looked at the door longingly, grinning his loose grin at Virginia, swinging his shoulders and knees, like he was already on his way.

But where was he headed? Virginia remembered Frank Baxter's voice on the phone this morning: "You don't believe he's doing it, and I'm *trying* not to believe it. But what if we're both wrong, and they catch him at it? They'll lock him up someplace for the rest of his life."

She stared into Jimmie's eyes, trying to divine the truth. His bright light gaze was steady and open as a child's. And it came to her that she'd been talking to the wrong person.

"I know," she began, matter-of-fact. "About the fires."

He stopped his restless movement, his eyes on her face.

"You know who's starting them?" she asked, in an easy, curious tone.

He turned and looked outside, nodding, grinning.

"Who is it, Jimmie?"

He glanced back at her, a little red spark in each eye. "The Australians," he said, in a soft secret voice. He put his head back and laughed, that same old long loud high silly laugh that used to make her kids laugh with him so, when they were all little. It sounded awful, coming out of him now.

She saw him, for a second, the way his neighbors would see him—this big grown man wandering around loose, laughing and talking crazy, while fires broke out all around him.

Then she raised her eyebrows encouragingly. "That's right," she went on. "The Australians. And you know who those Australians are, don't you?"

He reared back and opened his mouth, set to laugh again. But he clamped his lips shut and switched his head back and forth, staring at the ceiling.

"You don't know? Well, the Sheriff does," she said.

He picked one shoulder up and tucked his head in it, like he was hiding. She stepped closer to him. "The Sheriff says—" she spoke quietly, holding his eyes—"he knows who the Australians are. And if they do it again, they're going to jail."

He folded up small, like something hit him in the middle. "Going to jail?" he whispered, sucking in his breath.

"If they ever do it again," she repeated slowly, nodding with the words.

Aline came back in the room just then, waving his hat. "Got it," she called out, almost cheerful.

He scrunched his hat on and was out the door. She and Aline stood together at the front window and watched him start up the road—still walking hard, still carrying his tobacco stick, but with his head cranked down sideways now, his eyes on the ground.

"I'm so scared for him," Aline moaned, hunching forward, her arms clutching her belly. "All the time."

Virginia saw another little line of chin under Aline's chin quivering. She saw her friend, already beginning to be old, struggling for her great big child, like he was still inside of her, and she'd never get him out.

She couldn't say, "That's just Aline," either. Didn't she herself sometimes feel that same helpless clench of love and fear for her own smart, grown-up, out-there-on-their-own children? Wasn't part of her still laboring with her babies? All the time?

A car went by on the road. Jimmie poked his head up. He waved his tobacco stick.

Virginia laughed, leaning her shoulder against Aline's. "He's a good little old kid," she said. Aline swung to her, tears springing in her eyes, and they hugged, a strong hard bonafide hug this time.

———

Everybody kept waiting on the next fire. After a while, the Sheriff began telling folks he'd solved the crime—got it all taken care of, nice and quiet, nobody hurt. He never said how he'd done that, or who it was, but they were so grateful not to have the fires any more, they didn't care a darn.

Then it misted a little rain. And all along the burnt ridges, out from under the blackened fields and trees, bright green shoots of new grass appeared, startling, deliberate-looking, like they'd been sown there, and so alive, and so quick, like the fires had invited them.

# GAWAIN

## AND THE

# HORSEWOMAN

The great haunches coming up out of the creek, dripping, greyed over with the water. At the farther edge, she turned and looked back at Gawain with one big dark eye, coolly. Then moved off silently into the forest. He crossed the creek and followed her.

The most beautiful mare he'd ever seen, he said to himself, and not a sign of a saddle or bridle on her. Pure white. A fine head, high withers, a strong shoulder; and she was long and deep, all her lines flowing together smoothly. A step like a dancer, neck drooping, easy.

Following the mare now through twilight meadows. It was a matter of faith to see her—the almost-shape, as if the mist thickened a little, there. If he looked hard at what he saw, he wouldn't see it any more. But he found, sometimes, the cut line of a fresh hoof-print in a damp patch of dirt, or a steaming pile of dung. As night came on, he tracked her by ear, waiting for a far-off snort or sigh, then moving toward the sound, till the mist held still under his eye again; something seemed to have just dissolved, there. He didn't try to catch her, knowing how hard it is to approach any horse in the fog. He just wanted not to lose her altogether.

At daylight, she was not fifty feet from him, looking up at him thoughtfully as she grazed. He turned his back and began to search the ground, bent over from the waist. He moved slowly, head down, arms down, weighty, as if uprightness were not a habit he'd ever cultivated. He didn't listen for her. Instead he concentrated on the juicy mat of turf before him, where hop clover and dandelion spikes and yarrow tangled together. He picked one and then another. He pretended there was no creature here but him. And the world looked delicious to him, edible, for he hadn't eaten much in the last day. He sniffed at a chicory flower, turned up his lip at dock and sorrel. And elegantly nipped off dandelion greens with his front teeth.

At last he heard a snuffing; just behind him, her silvery nose nuzzled curiously the herbs at his feet. He squatted down and picked a handful, raised it to his mouth, sniffed it. Finally he felt her warm breath on his neck.

But when he made to turn a little and offer his green handful to her, she stepped back, stared at him. And was off again, at her steady pace. She didn't run from him—she only walked away. He wasn't sure just where he was any more, but he could tell he was descending. And from the clarity of the air, the distancing of the light, he knew she was leading him toward the sea.

Shade up ahead.

And that strange sense of something startling, but that it belonged there, it fit, as if it had grown up out of the ground. Under big trees, a shadowy troop of horses, three deep here and six deep there, a silent gathering. They stood still, their noses to the trees as if asleep, but their little furry ears were turning about alertly.

The white mare had already disappeared into the herd—at least, he couldn't pick her out. For they were all like her, all deep and fine. He wandered, half-dazed by all the silken flesh before him, down the hill. And saw a white sand track winding between two green turf walls, and below it, at a distance, the long green roofs of a house against the reach of the sea.

And a figure coming from the house—a tall boy, striding up the hill easily. The figure stopped, stared over at the horses, then came toward him. He saw it was not a boy but a woman dressed in a tunic and leggings—slim and brown, her dark hair clipped straight across by her ear. "She came back," the woman said. "I knew she would." She smiled in an easy way, though the smile seemed more for the mare than for him.

"She goes off on her own, then?" he asked.

"All the time." She looked him over, as if considering for the first time who he might be. "I hope she didn't cause you too much trouble."

"No trouble," Gawain said. He was a little flustered. He'd followed the mare all this way only to return her to her rightful owner, it seemed. And he'd never seen a woman in leggings before, or one that met his eye so steadily. Her eyes were startling in her dark face, light blue with a darker blue ring around the iris, so he kept feeling he was stepping off into something deep whenever he glanced at her. "I thought she'd come *looking* for me, somehow," he added. "I'd never seen anything like her."

"There isn't anything like her. Mean—?" she shook her head proudly .

"The truth is," he went on, "I never saw anything like any of these horses. What are they? Where did they come from?"

"Here," she said, with a little ambiguous gesture of her hand that suggested the woods, the fields, even the sea.

"What are they for? They're so beautiful. But you couldn't ride one in a battle. You couldn't plough with one, or pull a cart. What are they for?"

"Does everything have to be *for* something?" she said, as she led him over the hill. The farm stretched itself on the verge—at the edge of every field, the opening of the sea. He could hear it, faintly, washing against rocks below, and the call of gulls came up strangely through the reeling of the larks.

They went downhill toward the green roofs, which seemed to run right into the ground behind the house. A stone path wandered around the house to the apparent edge of nothing. He could see no way of getting into the house except by the chimney. He had a wild thought, as they walked right out over the sea, the surf crashing deep below them, that she was going to push him off the edge, or just step off it herself, with that long easy stride, and expect him to follow. But she turned suddenly and ducked down stone steps.

And here was the house, built into the cliff, tucked between fields and sea. From inside you could see only the blue expanse of waves and horizon. It was all glass along the front, little prisms of windows.

"She's home," sang the young woman as she stepped in the door.

"Ah good," came another woman's voice, deeper but with the same singing tone. Gawain bowed as a white-haired lady appeared, dressed in a gown.

"And brought someone with her."

"Is that you?" the older woman asked him. "Or your horse? She sometimes brings horses back."

"I guess she took one look at our horses and knew not to," he said, grinning. "She makes them all look gross or dumpy."

"She does have excellent judgment, by and large," the older woman said, looking Gawain up and down exactly as if he were a horse, so openly that he began to blush. He was glad, for once, to be toothy and long-legged.

"Well, I can't say she picked me out, exactly," he said. "I've been more of a . . . traveling companion."

"That's all *anybody* is. With her."

"Does she never lead any of yours astray?" he asked.

"Oh they know not to go with her. You can't count on her to show you the way back."

Gawain wondered if they were still talking about a horse. He stared out the windows at the sea. "It's a wonderful lookout," he said. "But don't you ever want to see the horses from the house? To watch over them?"

"Oh we do," said the older woman. "We do."

"Surely they're never . . ." He pointed down the cliffs, to the narrow strand of sand and grey rocks far below, "down there?"

"Well no," she said. "Except in the dark of the moon, perhaps. And then we couldn't see them, could we? But—" she laid her hand on his arm confidingly "—did you never see the horses' heads, with their manes all silver, rising above the great combers on full-moon nights?"

Gawain had a sudden vision of it, as if from memory, as she spoke. "Why yes—I have seen that. How very extraordinary. I never thought of it, but I have seen it. I figured no one else did, I suppose."

"We see them all the time," said the older woman. "On full-moon nights, the water comes almost up to our windows. On stormy nights, the foam flies against the glass. Perhaps we'll have a storm for you, while you're here."

"Oh no, I don't think so," said the younger one, as if that were too much to hope for.

There was a silence. Gawain looked from one woman to the other, and they looked back at him, as if they expected him to ask them something.

But all the usual questions—"Do you two live here alone?"—
"What is your father's name?"—even "How long have you been
here?"—seemed presumptuous. He settled for giving them his
name; the older woman nodded, introducing herself as Maude,
and the younger woman as her sister, Dana.

"Perhaps we can have a race," said Maude, at last, as if she
were thinking what they could have instead of a storm.

"*That* we might do," said Dana.

"I'll go and speak with her right now," Maude said,
disappearing up the steps.

"I'll ride Spotty Molly. If she goes," Dana called after her.
Turning back to Gawain, "Molly's a delicate sort." She looked
him up and down as the other one had. "You must weigh at least
two stone more than I do. But we can allow for that. There's
Snake Ears, he's a big stout horse, for all his small ears. And
Sunjumper could carry you easily. And Dropmyshoe, he's quick at
the mark under any weight. We'll give you your choice, of course.
But I'd take Sunjumper if I were you. He's not as stout as the other
two, but his stride is longer. He should be running at the end."

Now Gawain saw the meaning of the long circular track
inside the old turf walls. "Do you both race—against each other,
I mean?" Maude looked a little old for that, but these women
seemed capable of anything.

"Why no," Dana said. "They do the racing, you know. The
horses."

He laughed a little, not sure if it were a joke or not. "But you
do ride them?"

"Oh. As far as that goes—I'll certainly ride one of them."

Maude came back in, breathless. "It's all settled."

"What! Did you poll the whole herd already?" Gawain said,
wanting to enter into the spirit of things.

"Well, I asked *her*, anyway. We wouldn't want to have it
without *her*."

"And what did she say?"

"She's planning to be here. At least that long."

"How long is that?" Gawain asked.

"Till the night of the next full moon, of course."

Gawain stared at Dana. "You race them after dark? Isn't that dangerous?"

"Why no," she replied. "I don't think so. And it's the only time they'll run, in this kind of weather."

"But...how can you see where you're going? Or who wins?"

"They see, you know. So you don't need to."

Gawain began to wonder what he'd gotten himself into. He was a bold, heady rider, but he didn't much like the idea of riding a strange horse full-tilt down a narrow path after dark— and he'd seen that part of the track ran against an old stone foundation right on the edge of the sea. It was true that horses can see very well in the dark. But he was used to telling his horse where to go, not the other way around. "How far do you go?"

"Oh—once or twice around. Whichever suits you."

"Twice would be nice," he said, reasoning that he would rather go further, but slower, in the dark.

"Twice would be nice," the two women said, nodding at each other, agreeably.

He didn't want to be shown up as afraid, when Dana wasn't at all. Of course, they were her horses, he said to himself, and she apparently had done it before. He tried to imagine it— running the horse at a great clip inside the curve of the turf wall, then the hush of the sea suddenly below, from the height of the horse only that much further down. The white track ahead, like a line drawn at the edge of the world.

He found, over the next weeks, that he could very well imagine her doing it. He could not so easily imagine himself. But he thought of her every night, of riding a race against her, head to

137

head, the plunging shapes of the horses under them, her hands before her pushing on the moon-bright mane. And he thought it might be worth the rush along the falling-off edge of the cliff to see her—her long legs divided by the bulk of the horse, pressed to its side—whipping and driving, as she stared with her steady eyes that did not ask to see, only that the horse carry her quickly. Her eyes, being blue and then bluer, made him feel that he wanted to plunge into something. Her easy direct smile made him forget, sometimes, to hold himself back as he looked at her in the way he was used to do, with ladies, and then he found himself that much further into the depths of her gaze, as if he had started in deep, and gotten in deeper. He liked the way her short hair brushed the tips of her ears, he liked the slender brown neck that stretched above her tunic and the white smooth skin just at its edge, he liked her long legs that stalked about in a horsey way themselves. He liked Maude, too. She had more to say than Dana, and an odd way of saying it. But he liked the younger woman's silences even better than the older one's words.

He helped Dana, every day, feeding and watering, brushing the horses. But it was clear that she didn't need his help—she'd been doing it all this time by herself, and sometimes he felt more in the way than anything else.

Still, he told himself, the race had been arranged, so apparently he was expected to stay, at least that long. The truth was, of course, he never considered leaving.

He found himself, sometimes, almost wishing for some threat to the quiet of the little farmstead, so that he might be of use in defending it—for a big cat preying on the foals?—but no, he couldn't wish that—for an awful giant trying to carry off the younger woman on his horse?—but, he figured, she'd just jump on one of her own horses and be gone. What giant could catch her?

For he had seen all the horses move, by now. They mostly

slept in the shade of the trees all day, with brief excursions when a fly got after one of them. But every first step they took, every poise and movement they made, was—like the movements of the white mare—in a different category of quickness than the horses he was used to.

And on nights when the smell and sound of the sea came up with the fog and filled the house, there would be another sound, a sound he could never believe he was actually hearing, since it always seemed to be inside him, at first—and yet it would startle him out of sleep. A soft dull music from the earth, as if it moved and spoke, like the sea. But all around him, in the air. And he could see them, in his mind's eye, running together in the dark—intent, massed, flashing heavy through the thick air, with that sound like his heart beating.

He wondered if Dana woke and listened as they ran. He wanted to go and see if she indeed slept in her room at the other end of the long house; sometimes he doubted she did. Sometimes he thought she was out there, watching with her steady eyes, seeing them through the fog and the wind. Sometimes he thought she was on the back of one of the horses, running with them where they saw to run, readying them and herself for the night of the full moon. But he'd fall asleep again before he ever got up to see. Except for those wide-awake moments, he slept here as he had never slept before, with the sound of the sea calling him to it, lifting him up in great waves, pulling him down. And woke to the morning silence of the horses, and of Dana, who said nothing at all then, as opposed to the rest of the day, when she said almost nothing.

The two women seemed to have no curiosity about him. It was as if his life had begun, as far as they were concerned, when he appeared on their place. And he himself thought every morning his first, trudging up and down the hills to tend the horses with his long-legged companion. "The two of you would make one good horse," Maude said once, as they headed up to feed the herd. And he knew which end he'd be. She was always out in front of him with her long stride, easing up the hills before he'd caught his breath. They were out before light every day, when the dew still shone on the hedge parsley as the horses munched it, and she herself silvered over with the mist, her brown skin illuminated, her dark hair like a iron helmet washed with silver.

She seemed to have as little in common with other women he'd known as these horses had with other horses. She thanked him for his help, always, gave him her attention when he spoke to her, and otherwise paid him no mind.

Like the white mare, who never looked at him now. He saw her in the evenings, sometimes, when he went out alone—grazing by herself at a distance, with that lit-up look she'd had from the beginning. In the days, he couldn't spot her, and would ask, "Which one is she?" and Dana would peer at the herd and say, "Oh, she's *in* there."

The talk at dinner was of grass, herbs, hooves, water, corn, rain, drought, some new seaweed they were feeding the foaling mares, flies, manes, teeth, whether the ground was too hard or too soft, and the events of the farm world—a hawk sighted that day, a snake in the cellar, a strange hound or wolf-shape in the dawn light. And mostly tales of particular horses, how Ringtail had taken up with Longnose though they were old enemies, how Ragamuffin's new foal had kicked its mother, and a great many conversations reported between horses as overheard by Maude, who spent her afternoons wandering among the herd, talking to them at length.

"And then Lalala said, 'You do that and you'll be a three-legged horse from now on.'

"And Quickety-quick said, 'I believe that's my corn you're eating.' And then they were at it." She'd even provide the grunts and thumps, whinnies and snorts, warning roars, teeth snapping together, and a startling impression that she had just pinned her own ears.

Every day he felt himself privileged to be in this world, to be touching the great wide-eyed creatures, to be brushing their manes to one side of their long necks, to be feeding them corn from his hand. They did not come to him, still, as they did to Dana, crowding around her till she disappeared among them. But by now they would stand quietly when he approached, and let him hold them as she handled them. In the beginning they had been all staring eyes and flared nostrils and heads lunging this way and that, startled by this stranger in their midst. He felt proud to be accepted, now, at least as a friend of a friend. Still, he wondered if any one of them would ever let him ride it. He longed to do that, to feel a part of these beautiful beasts, moving as they moved.

"Shouldn't I be getting on one of them?" he asked Dana, one day, politely. "To get them used to it?"

Dana looked at him gravely. "Used to it?"

"For the race, I mean?"

"Oh. They're quite used to being ridden." He wondered how they could be. He'd seen her, sometimes, coming back in the mornings with a little stick in hand. But how could she exercise all of them by herself?

"Well," he said, not wanting to disagree, or look too careful. "But I'm not used to them, you see. Or they to me."

"Oh they'll do fine," she said, shaking her head proudly. "And as for you—" she looked him up and down in that way they both did "—you're a horseman, aren't you?"

He chose to feel complimented by this offhand description of himself, assuming he could manage whatever horse he found himself on. He'd always been able to, in fact. "Still, I've never ridden horses like these."

"Oh, they're easier than the other sort. You don't have to guide them. You just have to hang on."

Gawain was not reassured by this description. But he didn't feel free to question her further. He would have to have faith in her, as well as in the horses, apparently. And for some reason he did, though he was too good a horseman, ordinarily, to risk himself on a strange horse unless he *knew* it had been ridden recently. Dana said they had been, so he assumed they had, somehow—or that the one she'd pick out for him would have been, anyway. For he did not mean to choose—he meant to let her choose one for him. He was actually looking forward, by now, to the night of the full moon. He wanted to see what was happening, on those foggy nights—to be part of that sound that he heard now not only in his dreams, but over the surf and wind, as if the earth spoke to him, softly, at odd moments of the day. He wanted to be out alone with her in the dark, with the great shining creatures lifting them together toward the rush of the sea.

She never cursed the horses, he noticed, the way most men did who worked with horses. When they were difficult, she laughed and spoke to them warmly, as if she were entertained by such behavior. Sometimes a horse moved suddenly and pressed the two of them together, her body flexible against his. But her attention seemed always for the horse.

He thought to tell her about her twice-blue eyes, how he could not stop looking into them. But the words never quite came out. For one thing, he'd be discussing the obvious. He'd been looking into her eyes ever since he'd first seen them. He never saw any darkening there, any turning away, any flutter of the lashes that indicated he might be looking—or seeing—too much. Her gaze was still frank, calm, alert. And deep. Too deep to see into, without losing himself utterly. For that was the truth—she looked him down, every time.

If women were confusing to him before—and they had been—now he was lost indeed, presented with a woman who apparently wanted nothing in the world from him but that he would ride in a race against her. Something in him warred with the idea of doing *anything* against a woman—he'd always been inclined to do things *for* them. But he meant to oblige her in that way, since he couldn't in any other. That was one reason he had come to look forward to it—he would feel then he was at last doing something she actually wanted him to do.

He puzzled, occasionally—would she want him to lose the race, to oblige her? But one look at her steady blue eyes told him there were no games to be played. He could oblige her only by riding his hardest. Sometimes it seemed to him she was already in the race, her eyes set and still, her body, as she moved among the horses, relaxed but ready for anything, unstartleable. It was painful to him to think how, when the time came, he must overcome all that certainty. At the same time, he couldn't wait to do it.

For he assumed that he would win, of course. Could win, anyway, if he chose to. Wasn't he, as she had said, a horseman?

He sat with the two sisters one night and watched the almost-full moon rising over the sea. The three of them sat in perfect silence, comfortably, as if they were listening to music—and indeed they were, the wind and the tides rose higher every night, and the sea sang to them now, clearly, not that husky murmur he'd heard at the beginning. And he was sad, suddenly, wondering what would become of him after full moon—after the race was over. No one had ever spoken of *after* the race. He must go on, then, he supposed, continue on his way and see what it brought him. The women sat on either side of him, their heads tipped back with an identical gesture, the light of the moon on the sea flooding up into their faces, changing them to pure, severe masks. They looked at that moment of an age, neither of them young, and neither old. Maude spoke, at last, in her deeper voice, as if she'd read his thoughts: "Ah, but we wish you could stay here, Gawain, and be our stranger forever."

"Your stranger?" he said, stirring himself, smiling at her uncertainly. "Is that what I am?"

"What you have been, anyway," she said. "These last weeks."

"But if I did stay," he said, "you'd get used to me. I shouldn't be a stranger any more."

She turned to him and shook her head, with the sea glow running back and forth in her eyes. "All men are strangers here," she said.

He wasn't sure just what she meant. But as she said it, he felt so sad he knew it was true.

"Have there been other strangers here, before me?"

The women looked at each other, once.

"None we can remember," said Dana.

The next three days, as he worked beside her in the fields, were a terrible mixture of pain and pleasure to Gawain. He kept thinking of her words. And he kept seeing her here, forever, after he left, doing all these same things without him as she had done them before—speaking to the horses, walking up the hill in the morning, shaking out the corn into the crib. And not even remembering that he wasn't there to do them with her. And yet to be here with her now, to watch her body in its perfect relation to the horses, was so exquisite to him, thinking he should never see her again, that he wanted only to regard her, and never to think of what came next.

Sometimes, when she was walking just ahead of him, he imagined himself catching her gently by her shoulders, just there at the square outside points of them, pulling her lightly against him, putting his face down against her smooth brown neck. But he was not a man to take hold of a woman for the first time with her back turned. And he knew, anyway, that she would face around and look at him. And he never could imagine what would happen next.

The day of the race he spent lying in the grass near the cliff's edge, watching the sky open above him endlessly, as the sea opened below. He felt sick and dizzy, as if he'd been staring down into the waves for too long. He fell asleep, at last, out there, and woke to a warm breath on his face. The white mare was standing over him. He felt her velvet muzzle on his neck, saw her great dark eyes, with their long white eyelashes, looking into his. "Ah you beautiful creature," he said, tears coming to his eyes. "Why did you ever bring me here? Will *you* remember me when I go?"

"She may just." A high clear voice from behind the mare.

He turned his face away, embarrassed and miserable. But he felt the light touch on his neck again, repeated, tickling, till he laughed a little, and looked around. Dana was lying on the grass beside him, also staring at the sky, a long plume of grass-seed between her teeth. "She remembers everything," she said, the plume of grass bobbing as she spoke. She glanced over at him, smiling around it, brightly, easily. And it occurred to him that the last light touch he'd felt had perhaps been her brushing him with the grass.

Oh then he did look all the way into her eyes, unable at last to keep himself from it.

The pure plunge of coolness, light, like moving into another medium, where all was slow and unspoken. No concealment, but depths, far-off space, too transparent to penetrate with the eye. And something seemed to envelop him, a still calm giving-way resistance. It was as if he were being taken in by a different world, and breathing its pure atmosphere—or holding his breath for fear of breathing it.

He craned upward, trying to catch his breath, pretending to

be looking for the white mare, for she was gone now. "Will she come back to see us race tonight?" he said, needing to say something.

"She's got to. We can't do it without her."

"Why—is one of us going to ride her?"

She laughed a long laugh. "We don't ride *her*," she said. Then went on, after a moment, "She has a family interest, anyway. Molly's her daughter."

Gawain nodded. Molly had the same fine head, though not her dam's size and strength. "And my horse?" For it was settled that he was to ride Sunjumper.

"Oh, he just followed her home one day."

"Like me."

"Like you."

"But he got to stay."

"Yes. Well, he's here on trial, actually."

"You mean . . . if he wins tonight . . . he gets to stay?"

"May get to. It's just the first test."

"I'll do my best for him, then," he said, grinning at her, flashing a challenge with his eyes. For it had occurred to him, in a flash of hope, that perhaps he was on trial, too.

She grinned back at him, with a meaning gleam in her own eye. "Just be sure you let him do his best for you. He's the one doing the running."

The moon rose round and slow, and the seas rushed in, fell back, rushed in again. The whole great room of the house, the ceiling especially, was lit with the floating glow of the water, like an underwater chamber.

"We'll wait till the moon clears the roof," said Maude.

But a few minutes later she clapped her hands. "I do believe we're going to have a storm, after all," she said, as if it were the best news possible.

He heard, just then, a long low sound out of rhythm with the beating of the waves on the cliffs below. And the sky was figured with the pink bloom of the lightning. The voice of the sea grew deeper as they sat around the table. Both women were very animated, their faces rosy in the lightning's glow. Gawain had eaten and drunk lightly, as had Dana, he noticed. So it was a serious occasion, after all.

The moon was still clear, but a long black squall line showed itself, down to the south. Still the women waited, leisurely, watching the lightning flashes running toward the moon. "Perfect," Maude said, standing up, as the black cloud was silver-edged at last, and the wind lifted the spray and flung it against the glass.

"We don't want to get wet," said Dana; and they ran up the steps to the outside, laughing startlingly, high and low musical laughter in the storm's teeth.

Gawain stepped out behind them, and understood, as the wind shoved him back, just what the night promised. He got a glimpse of the sea, which seemed wonderfully high, the white lines of the surf rushing close below the fields, with the wind moving between like a solid force, in fists and hammers, whips and wings. Singing up high now like a cat, now sinking into the deeper roar of the waves, doubling and redoubling it. Everything went sideways, they all walked that way, crabbing along at an angle to the wind, pieces of spray blowing past them. He couldn't imagine they would even find the horses out there, much less ride them. But he hoped, against all reason, they would. The wind lifted him, and the clouds went by so fast, so fast, and he wanted to go that fast with them, the whole sky sliding over him as he went.

And then there was that other sound, the sound he still couldn't believe he heard, and it pulled him, under the wind and now the rain and the crash of thunder—that soft dull humming in the air, in the earth. And the horses in a flash of lightning, outlined, white, reaching into the dark, looking into it, intent, looking for them, for him. Then gone again. Crack in the black of the world. The two women made their way steadily against the storm, glancing at each other occasionally, serious now. The horses were just over there. Now they were here, bearing down on them, silent in the wind. And gone again. But the women marched up the hill, not even looking. And there they were again, under the dark edge of the trees as if they'd been there all along, just floating shadows at first, then the long shapes shifting, trading places, and then the shining bodies appearing, close up. To hand.

Lit by the lightning-glow, Spotty Molly and Sunjumper, wide-eyed, arch-necked, coming noses down looking for them, breathing in gusts like the wind. They stood, trembling all over, let the light bits of tack be put on them, and let themselves be led, swirling sideways, heads flung up, teeth showing, each foot lifted up too-high as if the ground were hot, to the place inside the turf wall that would serve as the starting point.

There was some protection here, where the wall curved out to the woods, so though the wind still whipped in their ears and they had to shout at each other close up how to go, it seemed almost a lull, compared to where they had been. And would go. Outside the turn of the wall, the world was a whirl, the white trace of the sand track a faint line curling into nothing where the dark wind overrode the hill. Maude put them both up. The great chalk eye of Sunjumper rolled back at Gawain desperately, as he snatched the horse's head to steady him for the start.

The wings of the sky clapped together once, and beyond was all that light. That much seeing too much, it dazzled his eyes, and he was blinded at the start. He never felt hooves meet ground, only felt the air shake with the lightning's crack, the horse lifted and strained to the sound as if cracked by a whip.

His hands he saw at last, holding hard the coarse mane. He could feel jolts of thunder and the world jumping with the lightning through the horse's body. He tried to see the white track ahead of him in the flashes, but all he saw was flying mane and foam and little bits of things the wind pitched at them.

Then there was Spotty Molly up ahead, he saw her in the next flash, she was quicker at the start as they had said, but he went after her now, no longer just hanging on, urging his horse forward with his hands and knees. Little pieces of sand came back in his face from Molly's flying hooves, ingrained themselves there as he pushed up closer to her. For a moment he thought Dana had fallen off at the start. Then he saw her slight shadow curved against the horse's back, riding low, almost invisible, except for her hands and arms, reaching and driving with the horse's motion. She stretched as the mare stretched, drew up as the mare drew up to gather herself for another stride, lengthened again as the mare reached out again. Her head disappearing into the mare's neck.

They were into the first turn, the wind right in his face, his teeth bared to meet it, his horse pulling harder.

He saw Molly's feet now, white and shell-shaped, flying up at him. Like the sea had flung them up. Eyes glanced back once from the darkness. He could hear the sea rushing to meet the land ahead, sounding higher than the wind.

The sound grew all around him. The air was full of water. Raindrops came hard as rocks. But he never heard them hit. The end of the turf wall ahead looked like the end of the world. They burst out of the containment of the curved wall, which had shouldered the wind off some, into the full force of the storm. The cut stones of the old foundation on the inside, and all else the sheer edge of the sea. The horses made the turn neatly, straightened out on the verge as if they had indeed been trained to do it. The wind pushed them close together. Gawain crouched low in the saddle as Dana did, feeling his horse's great rhythmic breathing as his own breath, its long striding legs a current flowing through him. On one side was the end of everything, white and black, water and air and fire all flinging themselves at him. On the other side was the dark huddle of earth, and here in between the narrow strand of life he held to, he felt himself alive in some way he'd never been before.

He saw clearly, in a lightning-flash, the sticks and mud inside Molly's left hind hoof, as his horse ranged up alongside her. They ran as a team toward the place where the track narrowed to fit itself into the turf wall again, his leg against Dana's leg, the horses' sides working together, breathing together, beating together the hearts of all. He glanced over in a flash of light and saw she was smiling her big smile, and her eyes were wide. Felt her breath rising and catching with his, with the motion of the horses, felt her narrow body rocking back and forth with his, bent and bent and bent, her arms reaching out and her little hips slung low and working easy and her legs folded tight on the smooth sides of the mare. And he longed for her, in that moment, for all of her, in a way he never had before, her length folded and unfolded, obedient to the horse's motion, flexible, half-kneeling, half-rising. He felt how light her weight, how fragile her bones against the powerful spring of her horse's ribs, how tenderly she bent to its neck, her small fists lost in its mane. He meant to ease past her gently, respectfully, as they came to the head of the turn. She glanced over at him, her eyes gleaming, dropped the mare's nose down into the narrowing track, and shot the gap, cutting from the outside to the inside, forcing him to give way just where the track narrowed into the turn, and was ahead of him again.

As they made the turn and crossed the start, there was another sound all around him, another flow from earth and sky. The other horses had joined them in the race. Waves of long necks working, mouths full of fire, wild eyes gleaming, the whole herd raced with them inside the narrow track. The sound he'd heard in his bed at night was all around him now, and his own heart's beating was indeed the sound itself. He was lost into the motion and the noise, the herd clambering up the sky, up the dark. Clouds of horses rushing by. His eyes felt as wide as they could be, seeing all around him black iron horses, molten in the lightning's glow, iridescent in the dark afterward. He could feel them all running under him, around him, with him, the shoulder of one horse against the shoulder of the next, leaning together into the turn of the wall. He'd lost all sense of his own body and was one of them, running as they ran, fluid, reaching, stretching out, lifting, lengthening, not man or beast but some creature of the elements, made of lightning's flare and the sound of the sea. He felt himself invisible at last, and felt other invisible riders beside him, guiding the other horses, eyes seeing as his saw in the dark, looking straight ahead but seeing all around, even up into the sky. As they made the turn again and came out into the tumult of the sea, the herd sheared off with the turf wall.

But he saw the waves come sweeping toward him with great dark heads rising from them, eyes green and glowing, the curling white foam now silver curling manes, long tails flaring out behind. He saw the great horses of the sea running with them, in company with them, their ranks rolling in like the surf. Their teeth were showing and their ears were pinned back and their crested necks arched like serpent's necks.

Spotty Molly was suddenly there ahead, dead-white in the lightning flash, he saw her running not on earth but on the fluid darkness of the seas, which lifted her in waves ahead of him. His own horse rode waves of air, lifted and lifted again. And suddenly all the others were gone, only the wind and rain around them, and she and he were still there, still that far apart, and he saw he must take her now on the verge, or the turn

151

would be on them and he would lose the race. The track was narrowing already, the edge that much nearer.

He drove the great chestnut forward, dropping his hands way down, and whistled shrilly in his horse's ear, to assure himself and the horse that he was real, it was real, and they were going to take it all now. But the horse was already reaching out, his big head dropped and his ears pinned back and he reached out, his stride stretched as thin as if he were a snake drawn along the track. As Gawain came to her again, he saw her soaked with the spray, her eyes almost shut, her mouth open, teeth white and set and her head up like a snake, shining all over silver, her hands scrubbing in the silver of Molly's mane. All of her arched upward, then straightened out, almost flat, worshipfully she bent herself again to the mare's neck, lengthening out of herself as she asked the mare to lengthen, her face buried in Molly's mane, fading again into the mare, the invisible rider. They were coming together into the turn.

And she wouldn't give him the way. He was on the outside, the white forelegs of his horse flashing against black nothing, the little mare, white in the dark and fragile, just ahead, and he saw eyes look back, once, and then the white butt drifted out, the gap closing up. He'd have to take her on the inside, he saw, here on the very edge of the cliff, where the track slanted toward the sea. He asked his horse again, telling it with his hands to trust him, driving it with legs and body and heart, and he took the inside against her, pulled up to her, and passed her, Molly's little head with its ears pinned falling away from him, the rider with her face in the mare's mane, still driving her for all she was worth, blindly. The mare's head disappeared from the corner of his eye, but he still seemed to hear hoof-beats close behind him in the dark. The shadow of the turf wall curving in from the outside now.

And then—his heart cold—he saw a white nose appearing

again in the corner of his eye. But he had her beaten, he told himself. She could come back at him now, with the track narrowing and him on the inside, but she could not cut the corner again and take it from him without going right through his horse. Still the white shape was inching up on him, the pale head shining, larger suddenly, and higher up. She was crowding him in, he felt the height of the stone wall on his inside, the stones clear and visible in a flash of light, each one separately, as if someone were throwing them at him. The mare's whole head in his vision now. She was not going to take back, he realized. There was room for only one horse, and the mare was coming on, she was running at the hole, with the sea beyond her, as if she could indeed run on the water and air as well as the earth. And he would have to let her win or let her fall. To take his horse up—and Sunjumper was running now straight out, full-stride, brave, strong, demanding to go on—give her room and lose the race, or lose her, let her go over the cliff. The shadow of the turf wall coming up fast now, curled like a tunnel, the one-horse hole, the wind hollowing into it, and he was screaming at her "Get back! Get back!" But he saw the mare's teeth shining in the dark, and he knew she wouldn't get back. And one jolt against his great long-striding beast would be enough to throw her off into the wind. His horse had the race won, if he stayed as he was, the mare was coming back but Sunjumper wasn't giving up, he was running strong, striding easy, and would not quit before the finish, Gawain knew, fighting with all his breath and heart for the right to stay there and win the race. He thought for a moment of snatching her off the mare to save them both, but Molly would surely go over, riderless, and she'd never forgive him that. And he'd never forgive himself. And she'd never forgive him for not letting her finish the race. And she'd never forgive him for not riding his hardest against her. He wondered wildly if she had some secret escape route, knew of some little path that went off around the turf wall safely. But he had been on that outside edge, and he knew there was nothing there but sheer drop.

At the last minute he stood upright in the saddle and yanked Sunjumper's head up, the chalk eye rolling around at him hopelessly, the horse going down at the shoulder, toward the rock wall. And as she flashed by he saw no rider there, only the great dark eye of the white mare looking round at him once. He threw all his weight the other way, but everything was slipping then. His horse twisted sideways, the narrow edge of sand exploding out from under them, powdering into the wind. The plunging forward, downward. Gawain held on, the mane turning liquid in his hands.

Blythe Jamieson

# The Author

**Susan Starr Richards** was born and raised in Winter Park, Florida, and has a B.A. from the University of Florida and an M.A. from the University of Washington. She taught for ten years at the University of Kentucky, and has spent the rest of her life raising racehorses and writing.

She has been a National Endowment for the Arts Fellow in Fiction, and has received a Kentucky Arts Council Fellowship. Her stories have been anthologized in *The O. Henry Prize Stories*, and in *Best New Stories from the South*, and have appeared in *The Kenyon Review*, *The Sewanee Review*, *Shenandoah*, *The Southern Review*, and in *Thoroughbred Times*, as winner of their first National Fiction Prize. Her essays have been published in *Ms. Magazine*, *Essence*, *New Woman*, and anthologized by Oxford University Press and The Odyssey Press. She was the 2004 Lecturer in American Literature at Doane College, Nebraska. Larkspur Press published *The Life Horse*, a book of poems, in 2005.

For twenty years, she did her writing at night, in the tack room of her barn, while waiting for various thoroughbred mares to foal. That worked well, except for the nights when the mares inconvenienced her by actually foaling. She and her husband have raised horses in the Inner Bluegrass—in Fayette County—and on its outer fringes, near the Harrison-Scott County line. The Kentucky country is still a little wild, some of the people are a little wild, and the horses have always been wild, so she's never had to look far for a good story.